W9-DEX-241

Author Chronologies

General Editor: **Norman Page**, Emeritus Professor of Modern English Literature, University of Nottingham

Published titles include:

Peter Preston
A D. H. LAWRENCE CHRONOLOGY

Nicholas von Maltzahn
AN ANDREW MARVELL CHRONOLOGY

Author Chronologies Series
Series Standing Order ISBN 0–333–71484–9
(*outside North America only*)

You can receive future titles in this series as they are published by placing a standing order.
Please contact your bookseller or, in case of difficulty, write to us at the address below with your
name and address, the title of the series and the ISBN quoted above.

Customer Services Department, Macmillan Distribution Ltd, Houndmills, Basingstoke, Hampshire
RG21 6XS, England

An Edith Wharton Chronology

Edgar F. Harden

First published in 2005 by
PALGRAVE MACMILLAN
Houndmills, Basingstoke, Hampshire RG21 6XS and
175 Fifth Avenue, New York, N.Y. 10010
Companies and representatives throughout the world.

PALGRAVE MACMILLAN is the global academic imprint of the Palgrave Macmillan division of St. Martin's Press, LLC and of Palgrave Macmillan Ltd. Macmillan® is a registered trademark in the United States, United Kingdom and other countries. Palgrave is a registered trademark in the European Union and other countries.

ISBN-13: 978–1–4039–9583–4 hardback
ISBN-10: 1–4039–9583–4 hardback

This book is printed on paper suitable for recycling and made from fully managed and sustained forest sources.

A catalogue record for this book is available from the British Library.

Library of Congress Cataloging-in-Publication Data
Harden, Edgar F.
    An Edith Wharton chronology / Edgar F. Harden.
        p. cm.—(Author chronologies)
    Includes bibliographical references and index.
        ISBN 1–4039–9583–4
        1. Wharton, Edith, 1862–1937 – Chronology. 2. Authors, American – 20th
    century – Chronology. I. Title. II. Author chronologies (Palgrave Macmillan
    (Firm))

PS3545.H16Z662 2005
813'.52—dc22   2005051383

10 9 8 7 6 5 4 3 2 1
14 13 12 11 10 09 08 07 06 05

Printed and bound in Great Britain by
Antony Rowe Ltd, Chippenham and Eastbourne

*For my son, Edgar and for my predecessors
in Wharton bibliographical and
biographical scholarship*

Contents

General Editor's Preface

Most biographies are ill adapted to serve as works of reference – not surprisingly so, since the biographer is likely to regard his function as the devising of a continuous and readable narrative, with excursions into interpretation and speculation, rather than a bald recital of facts. There are times, however, when anyone reading for business or pleasure needs to check a point quickly or to obtain a rapid overview of part of an author's life or career; and at such moments turning over the pages of a biography can be a time-consuming and frustrating occupation. The present series of volumes aims at providing a means whereby the chronological facts of an author's life and career, rather than needing to be prised out of the narrative in which they are (if they appear at all) securely embedded, can be seen at a glance. Moreover whereas biographies are often, and quite understandably, vague over matters of fact (since it makes for tediousness to be forever enumerating details of dates and places), a chronology can be precise whenever it is possible to be precise.

Thanks to the survival, sometimes in very large quantities, of letters, diaries, notebooks and other documents, as well as to thoroughly researched biographies and bibliographies, this material now exists in abundance for many major authors. In the case of, for example, Dickens, we can often ascertain what he was doing in each month and week, and almost on each day, of his prodigiously active working life; and the student of, say, *David Copperfield* is likely to find it fascinating as well as useful to know just when Dickens was at work on each part of that novel, what other literary enterprises he was engaged in at the same time, whom he was meeting, what places he was visiting, and what were the relevant circumstances of his personal and professional life. Such a chronology is not, of course, a substitute for a biography; but its arrangement, in combination with its index, makes it a much more convenient tool for this kind of purpose; and it may be acceptable as a form of "alternative" biography, with its own distinct advantages as well as its obvious limitations.

Since information relating to an author's early years is usually scanty and chronologically imprecise, the opening section of some volumes in this series groups together the years of childhood and adolescence. Thereafter each year, and usually each month, is dealt with separately. Information not readily assignable to a specific month or day is given as a general note under the relevant year or month. The first entry for each month carries an indication of the day of the week, so that when necessary this can be readily calculated for other dates. Each volume also contains a bibliography of the principal sources of information. In the chronology itself, the sources of many of the more specific items, including quotations, are identified, in order that the reader who wishes to do so may consult the original contexts.

NORMAN PAGE

Acknowledgements

Any scholar attempting to articulate the details of Edith Wharton's life and her extensive publications must inevitably be thankful for ensuing memoirs and scholarship, notably that of R. W. B. Lewis and Shari Benstock. I am especially indebted to his biography and his editions of the short stories and the letters, as well as to Stephen Garrison's invaluable *Bibliography*. I also offer very grateful thanks, as always, to Anita Mahoney of the Dean of Arts office, Simon Fraser University, for her computer assistance, and should like to express my gratitude for the editorial helpfulness of Paula Kennedy.

List of Abbreviations

Benstock	Shari Benstock, *No Gifts From Chance. A Biography of Edith Wharton* (New York: Scribner, 1994)
Glance	Edith Wharton, *A Backward Glance* (New York and London: Appleton-Century, 1934)
HJ Letters 4	*Henry James Letters*, ed. Leon Edel, Volume IV: 1895–1916 (Cambridge, Mass.: Harvard University Press, 1984)
Letters	*The Letters of Edith Wharton*, ed. R. W. B. Lewis and Nancy Lewis (New York: Scribner, 1988)
Lewis	R. W. B. Lewis, *Edith Wharton: A Biography* (New York, Evanston, San Francisco, and London: Harper and Row, 1975)
Price	Alan Price, *The End of The Age of Innocence. Edith Wharton and the First World War* (New York: St. Martin's Press)
Scribner	Charles Scribner's Sons

Introduction

One welcomes the opportunity to present a chronology such as this, offering as it does a format for an intense articulation of Edith Wharton's biographical experiences, which are presented amid the detailed unfolding of her imaginative writing, and set in the larger context of historical developments that impinged on her life. The scope of her experiences with other human beings is very impressive. The intensity of her efforts to honor them and herself is constantly evident, and her endless efforts to express her joyful and tragic experiences compel repeated admiration.

Edith Wharton was a prolific as well as an intensely committed writer, who created not only novels, novellas, tales, and poems, but also a notable series of appreciative travel writings reflecting her experiences especially in the United States, Britain, France, and Italy, and also wrote an autobiography and many letters. In addition, she translated works, participated in the theatrical presentations of her novels, wrote essays on other writers and their works, and wrote essays on the creation and criticism of fiction. Beyond all these manifold activities, she greatly contributed to the welfare of the unemployed, of suffering soldiers, and of refugees from warfare, by direct involvement, by raising funds, and by articulating wartime experiences in France and Belgium in a series of public appeals. The range of her energies was immense.

Ancestry and Family

The Joneses

A Jones ancestor arrived from England during the early eighteenth century and came to acquire land in New York City, where Edith Wharton's paternal grandfather, Edward Renshaw Jones, married Elizabeth Schermerhorn, member of a prominent family. Their son, George Frederick Jones, who had graduated from Columbia College, married Lucretia Stevens Rhinelander, also a member of a prominent New York family, on 17 October 1844. (Lewis 11–13)

The Stevenses

A Stevens forbear was settled in New England by the 1630's. Wharton's maternal great-grandfather, Ebenezer Stevens, served as an artillery officer during the Revolutionary War, after which he settled in New York, came to own a fleet of merchant ships, and became a member of the New York assembly. He married the daughter of a Hartford judge, Lucretia Ledyard, and sired eleven children, a number of whom made socially prominent marriages in New York, including their daughter, Mary Lucretia Lucy Ann Stevens, who married Frederic William Rhinelander. In turn, their daughter, Lucretia Stevens Rhinelander, was to be Edith Wharton's mother. (Lewis 8–11)

Chronology

1862–1937

1844

October

17 (Thu)   George Frederic Jones marries Lucretia Stevens Rhinelander at her parents' home in Hell Gate, north of New York City. After their honeymoon they move into their house at 80 East 21st St., in Gramercy Park, New York City. [Lewis 12]

1846

January

Birth of their son, Edith Wharton's brother, Frederic Rhinelander Jones ("Freddy"). [Lewis 12]

1850

May

29 (Wed)   Birth of their second son, Henry Edward Jones ("Harry"). [Lewis 15]

1851

December

2 (Tue)   Louis Napoleon's *coup d'état* ends the Second Republic.

1850's

The Joneses take a summer home at the small seaport town of Newport, Rhode Island. [Lewis 15]

1860

November

20 (Tue)   Abraham Lincoln is elected President of the United States.

December

20 (Thu)   South Carolina adopts an Ordinance of Secession.

1861

April

12 (Fri)   Southern rebels fire on Fort Sumter, South Carolina, beginning the American Civil War.

15   Lincoln issues a call for 75,000 volunteers.

1862

January
24 (Fri)   Birth of Edith Newbold Jones in New York City. [Lewis 5]

April
20 (Sun)   Edith is christened in Grace Church, New York City. [Lewis 5]

1863

January
1 (Thu)   Lincoln issues the Emancipation Proclamation.

July
1 (Wed)   Beginning of the decisive battle of Gettysburg, which ends on the 3rd after Union forces defeat the Confederates.

1865

April
9 (Sun)   Lee surrenders to Grant at Appomattox, ending the American Civil War.
14   Lincoln is assassinated by John Wilkes Booth. Andrew Johnson becomes President.

1866

November
            George and Lucretia Jones go to England with Edith and Harry, whom they enroll at Trinity College, Cambridge. The parents and Edith then travel to France and ultimately to Rome, where they spend a year. [Lewis 17]

1868

            After a trip through Spain from which, Edith later said, "I brought back an incurable passion for the road," the parents and Edith settle in Paris for two years. [Lewis 17; *Glance* 31]

1870

July
19 (Sun)   Beginning of the Franco-Prussian War. The Joneses are in the Black Forest. [Lewis 18]

August

In Bad Wildbad, Edith contracts typhoid fever and is severely ill. [Lewis 18]

September

The Joneses move to Florence. [Lewis 18]

October

2 (Tue) Rome is made the capital of a united Italy.

1871

January

28 (Sat) Paris capitulates and an armistice with Germany is signed.

March

18 (Sat) A commune is established in Paris.

May

10 (Wed) Franco-German Peace of Frankfurt is signed, France ceding Alsace-Lorraine to Germany.

21–28 "Bloody Week" in Paris ends with the defeat of the commune.

August

31 (Thu) L. A. Thiers is elected French President.

1872

June

The Joneses return to New York and then Newport, staying at their home on the island of Pencraig. By this time Edith has gained knowledge of French, German, and Italian. For the next number of years New York and Newport are the poles of her life. [Lewis 19]

1876

Autumn

Edith begins her first piece of extended fiction, "Fast and Loose," which she completes in January 1877, but does not attempt to publish. She also writes poetry. [Lewis 30–31]

1877

April

24 (Tue)   Russia declares war on Turkey, raising tensions in England and Europe.

1878

March

3 (Sun)   The Treaty of San Stefano is signed (ratified on 23 March), ending the Russian-Turkish War of 1877–78.

Fall

Mrs. Jones has a selection of Edith's poems privately printed in Newport. Entitled *Verses*, it contains "Le Viol d'Amour," "Vespers," "Bettine to Goethe," "Spring Song," "Prophesies of Summer," "Song," "Heaven," "Maiden, Arise," "Spring," "May Marian," "Opportunities," "The Last Token," "Raffaelle to the Fornarina," "Chriemhild of Burgundy," "Some Woman to Some Man," "Lines on Chaucer," "What We Shall Say Fifty Years Hence, of Our Fancy-Dress Quadrille," "Nothing More," "June and December," "October," "A Woman I Know," "Daisies," "Impromptu," "Notre Dame des Fleurs," and German translations: "Three Songs from the German of Emanuel Geibel," "Longing" (from the German of Schiller), and "A Song" (freely translated from the German of Rückert).

1879

May

30 (Fri)   "Only a Child" [poem], New York *World*, p. 5.

December

Edith makes her social debut, coming out at a ball given by the millionaire's wife, Mrs. Levi Morton, at her home on Fifth Avenue near 42nd St. in New York City. [Lewis 33]

1880

February

"The Parting Day" [poem], *Atlantic Monthly*, 45: 194.

March

"Areopagus" [poem], *Atlantic Monthly*, 45: 335.

April

"A Failure" [poem], *Atlantic Monthly*, 45: 464–65.
"Patience" [poem], *Atlantic Monthly*, 45: 548–49.

May

"Wants" [poem], *Atlantic Monthly*, 45: 599.

July

Mr. and Mrs. Jones, Edith, and her first close young male friend, Harry Stevens, go for vacation to Bar Harbor, Maine. [Lewis 39]

November

Edith's father, because of failing health, is urged by his physician to go to southern France. After a brief stay in London, where Edith visits the National Gallery, the parents and Edith go to Cannes. [Lewis 42–43; *Glance* 85–86]

1881

Summer

The parents and Edith go to Bad Homburg, where her mother has been sent for a cure. [*Glance* 87]

July

2 (Sat) President James A. Garfield is fatally shot, and lingers until 19 September, when he is succeeded by Chester A. Arthur.

September

The parents and Edith are in Venice, where they are joined by Harry Stevens. [Lewis 43]

1882

January/February

The parents and Edith return to Cannes, accompanied by Harry Stevens. [Lewis 43]

March

George Frederic Jones dies at Cannes. Lucretia and Edith return to Newport, as does Harry. From her father's will, Edith receives $20,000 outright and a share of the considerable inheritance that is placed in a trust fund that provides her with a good income. [Lewis 44, 47–48]

August

Edith and Harry agree to become engaged, but his mother refuses her consent, and the engagement plans are given up. [Lewis 44–46]

1883

July

In Bar Harbor, Edith meets Walter Van Rensselaer Berry, who had graduated from Harvard in 1881 and is now preparing for a legal career in Washington. They grow close, but do not become engaged. [Lewis 48–49]

August

In Newport, Mrs. Jones gives a dinner party for Edward Robbins Wharton, who had graduated from Harvard in 1873, had become a friend of Edith's brother, Harry, and had visited the Joneses on a number of occasions. He was a thirty-three year old man of leisure supported by his parents and living in Boston. [Lewis 50–51]

1884

February

Edward Wharton ("Teddy") comes to New York to escort Edith to the Patriarchs' Ball. [Lewis 51]

1885

March

Edith becomes engaged to Teddy Wharton. [Lewis 51]

April

29 (Wed) Edith and Teddy are married at Trinity Chapel in New York City, and have a wedding breakfast in the home of her mother, who is now living at 28 West 25th St. The Whartons then stay at a cottage on her mother's estate in Newport. For the next number of years they live at Pencraig Cottage from June to February, and from February to June travel in Europe. [Lewis 51, 54]

July

18 (Sat) Death of Harry Stevens. [Lewis 52]

1886

February
> The Whartons leave the United States to travel in Europe, especially Italy. They are accompanied by an old family friend of the Joneses, Egerton Winthrop, who has been sharing with Edith his love of literature and the fine arts, and introducing her to scientific thought as represented by writers like Darwin and Spencer. [Lewis 56–57, 60; Benstock 61–63]

1887

February
> The Whartons leave the United States to travel in Europe, especially Italy. They are accompanied by Egerton Winthrop. [Lewis 57; Benstock 63]

1888

February
17 (Fri) The Whartons begin a four-month tour of the Aegean on a rented yacht with Edith's friend, James Van Alen, a wealthy New York socialite. [Lewis 58; Benstock 64]

March
14 (Wed) A distant Jones relative dies, leaving a large legacy, from which Edith and her brothers each receive more than $120,000. [Lewis 59]

December
> The Whartons establish residence in New York City, renting a house on Madison Ave. [Lewis 60; Benstock 67]

1889

January
> Edith has three poems accepted for publication, including one at *Scribner's Magazine*, whose editor, Edward Burlingame, became a friend and mentor. She later wrote that he "became one of my most helpful guides in the world of letters." At this time he "not only accepted my verses, but (oh, rapture!) wanted to know what else I had written; and this encouraged me to go to see him, and laid the foundation of a friendship which lasted till his death." [*Glance* 109; Lewis 60]

October
> "The Last Giustiniani" [poem], *Scribner's Magazine*, 6: 405–06.

December
> "Euryalus" [poem], *Atlantic Monthly*, 64: 761.
> "Happiness" [poem], *Scribner's Magazine*, 6: 715.

1890

May
26 (Mon) Burlingame accepts Edith's first work of fiction to be published: "Mrs. Manstey's View." [Lewis 61]

1891

January
> "Botticelli's Madonna in the Louvre" [poem], *Scribner's Magazine*, 9: 74.

February
> "The Tomb of Ilaria Giunigi" [poem], *Scribner's Magazine*, 9: 156.

Spring
> The Whartons go to Paris, the French Riviera, Florence, and Venice. [Lewis 65]

May
22 (Fri) Teddy's father, William Craig Wharton, confined in a mental hospital near Boston, commits suicide. [Benstock 73]

July
> "Mrs. Manstey's View" [short story], *Scribner's Magazine*, 10: 117–22.

November
> "The Sonnet" [poem], *The Century Magazine*, 43: 113.
> Edith purchases for $19,670 a New York City house on Fourth Ave. near 78th St. (eventually designated 884 Park Ave.). [Lewis 67]

1892

November

"Two Backgrounds" [poem], *Scribner's Magazine*, 12: 550.

1893

January

"Experience" [poem], *Scribner's Magazine*, 13: 91.

March

Edith purchases a home for $80,000 in Newport, "Land's End." "I loved Land's End, with its windows framing the endlessly changing moods of the misty Atlantic, and the nightlong sound of the surges against the cliffs." She soon begins to redo the grounds and especially the house's interior, working with a young Boston architect and interior decorator, Ogden Codman, Jr. [*Glance* 106; Lewis 68]

Autumn

Paul Bourget, the French novelist and essayist, who is writing a series of articles on America, later to be collected in *Outre-Mer*, comes to Newport, where he spends three weeks with his wife, Minnie. They call on Edith at Land's End, repeatedly see each other, and thereby begin "our long friendship . . . a friendship as close with the brilliant and stimulating husband as with his quiet and exquisite companion." Edith was often to visit them in France. [*Glance* 103; Lewis 68–69]

September

"Chartres" [poem], *Scribner's Magazine*, 14: 287.

November

"The Fullness of Life" [short story], *Scribner's Magazine*, 14: 699–704.

24 (Fri) Burlingame writes to Edith offering to have Scribner publish a volume of her short stories. It was not to appear, however, until 1899. [Lewis 70]

Edith closes "Land's End" and goes to Boston for two weeks with Teddy, visiting his mother, before going to New York, where she confers with Burlingame at the Scribner office. [Lewis 71]

December

The Whartons go to Europe, arriving in Paris after Christmas, and calling upon the Bourgets. [Lewis 71]

1894

March

The Whartons are in Cannes, and later that month go to Florence, where Edith brings a letter of introduction from Bourget to Violet Paget ("Vernon Lee"), the British-born critic of Italian art and architecture. In *A Backward Glance*, Edith singled out three of Paget's books that she already loved, *Studies of the Eighteenth Century in Italy, Belcaro: Being Essays on Sundry Aesthetical Questions*, and *Euphorion: Being Studies of the Antique and the Medieval in the Renaissance*, calling them "three of my best-loved companions of the road." She and Violet Paget were to become lifelong friends. [Lewis 71–72; *Glance* 130]

April

While exploring an obscure monastery in the countryside southwest of Florence, Edith sees terra cotta paintings that she recognizes as akin to the work of Giovanni della Robbia. She then has them photographed, sends the photos to the director of the Royal Museum, and ultimately has her attribution verified. She wrote about it in "A Tuscan Shrine." [Lewis 73]

May

"That Good May Come" [short story], *Scribner's Magazine*, 15: 629–42.

June

"Life" [poem], *Scribner's Magazine*, 15: 739.

Summer

Edith experiences a nervous collapse that lasts for many months, marked by nausea, fatigue, headaches, and severe depression. [Lewis 74]

October

"An Autumn Sunset" [poem], *Scribner's Magazine*, 16: 419.
Edith's brother, Freddy, and Elsie West are living in France as a married couple. [Benstock 82]

1895

January

"Jade" [poem], *The Century Magazine*, 49: 391.

"A Tuscan Shrine" [travel article], *Scribner's Magazine*, 17: 23–32.

February

The Whartons are in Europe with Egerton Winthrop. [Benstock 79, 82]

June

9 (Sun)   The Whartons return to Newport. [Benstock 80]

October

"The Lamp of Psyche" [short story], *Scribner's Magazine*, 18: 418–28.

December

15 (Sun)   Writing to Burlingame, Edith tells him that since she last wrote him "over a year ago," she has "been very ill" and has composed only "a little." [*Letters* 35]

1896

February

The Whartons go to Europe, travelling in France and especially in Italy, but also visiting Howard Sturgis in England. [Benstock 81]

March

16 (Mon)   Mary Cadwalader Jones secures a divorce in New York on the grounds of adultery from Edith's brother, Freddy, who is now living in Paris with a mistress. [Benstock 81]

Summer

Edith's brother, Harry, moves to Paris, where he resides at 146 Avenue des Champs Elysées. [Benstock 81]

July

Edith has largely recovered from her nervous collapse. [Lewis 77]

"The Valley of Childish Things, and Other Emblems" [short story], *The Century Magazine*, 52: 467–69.

October

The Whartons return to America, staying at Newport while their New York City house is being remodelled. [Benstock 81]

1897

July

Walter Berry arrives at Land's End, stays a month, and elaborately advises Edith about revising the draft of a book that she was working on with Ogden Codman, Jr., which became *The Decoration of Houses*. She also works with William Crary Brownell of Scribner. [Lewis 77]

December

3 (Fri)   *The Decoration of Houses* (New York: Scribner).
13   The Whartons move to their home in New York City. [Benstock 88]
           Burlingame asks Edith to translate three Italian stories. [Benstock 89]

1898

January

"Phaedra" [poem], *Scribner's Magazine*, 23: 68.
Edith's mother, Lucretia Jones, has moved to Paris and is living at 50 Avenue du Bois de Bologne near her two sons. [Benstock 83]

February

15 (Tue)   In Cuba, which is controlled by Spain, though it is in the midst of a rebellion, the *U. S. S. Maine* is blown up in the harbor of Havana, killing 260 crew members. The event leads to the Spanish-American War, which is formally declared by Congress on 24 April.

April

Walter Berry prompts the Whartons to visit Washington, where he is practicing law. There she meets and becomes "fast friends" with young George Cabot "Bay" Lodge, whom she finds exceptionally "brilliant and versatile." [Lewis 80; *Glance* 149]

May

The Whartons return to Newport. [Benstock 91]

June

The Decoration of Houses (London: Batsford).

July

"The One Grief" [poem], *Scribner's Magazine*, 24: 90.

August

Edith leaves Newport to visit her brother Freddy's former wife, Minnie, in Bar Harbor, Maine, but becomes severely depressed and does not write. [Lewis 82]

September

Edith makes a recovery, but then suffers a relapse. [Lewis 82]

10 (Sat) *Stories By Foreign Authors* (New York: Scribner). Edith did three translations: "A Great Day" [from Edmondo de Amicis] pp. 11–34, "It Snows" [from Enrico Castelnuovo] pp. 113–34, and "College Friends" [from Edmondo de Amicis] pp. 137–68.

October

31 (Mon) Edith goes to Philadelphia for a rest-cure and stays for several months at the Stenton Hotel, where she is treated by Dr. George McClellan. [Benstock 93–95]

November

"The Pelican" [short story], *Scribner's Magazine*, 24: 620–29.

1899

January

"The Muse's Tragedy" [short story], *Scribner's Magazine*, 25: 77–84.

The Whartons move to a rented house in Washington at 1329 K St., staying until May. [Lewis 84, 88]

March

The Greater Inclination (New York: Scribner). It contains eight short stories: "The Muse's Tragedy," "A Journey," "The Pelican," "Souls Belated," "A Coward," "The Twilight of the God," "A Cup of Cold Water," and "The Portrait."

The Greater Inclination (London: John Lane, The Bodley Head).

May

The Whartons are briefly in New York preparatory to leaving for Europe. After a short stay in London, they go to Paris for several weeks and then travel through France to Switzerland, where they stay at a wateringplace, Ragatz, joining the Bourgets. [Lewis 89]

August

The Bourgets return to Paris but then rejoin the Whartons at Lake Como and journey with them in "an old-time travelling carriage" through the northern Italian countryside. [Lewis 90–91; *Glance* 105]

September

The Whartons return to Newport. Shortly afterwards, they go to Lenox, in western Massachusetts, staying in the unoccupied summer home of Teddy's mother and sister. [Lewis 93]

October

9 (Mon)   Outbreak of the Boer War in South Africa, which lasts until May 1902.
The Whartons visit Teddy's brother William and his family in Groton, Massachusetts. [Benstock 108]

November

The Whartons return to Newport. [Lewis 94]

December

The Whartons return to 884 Park Ave. [Lewis 94]

1900

January

18 (Thu)   "April Showers" [short story], *Youth's Companion*, 74: 25–28.

March

"The Touchstone" [novella], *Scribner's Magazine*, 27: 354–72.
Writing to Sara Norton, Charles Eliot Norton's daughter, whom Edith had previously met and who had just sent an appreciative letter regarding "The Touchstone," Edith expresses her gratitude. They were to become close friends. [Benstock 111–12]

April

"The Touchstone," *Scribner's Magazine*, 27: 483–501.

2 (Mon)   "Frederic Bronson" [letter to the editor], *New York Evening Post*, p. 4.

The Touchstone (New York: Scribner).
A Gift From The Grave [*The Touchstone*] (London: Murray).

May

The Whartons leave for England, where they visit London and a number of country estates. [Lewis 96; Benstock 112–13]

June

" 'Copy': A Dialogue" [short story], *Scribner's Magazine*, 27: 657–63.
"In an Alpine Posting-Inn" [travel article], *Atlantic Monthly*, 85: 794–98.
The Whartons go to Paris, where they visit the Bourgets and attend a major international technological exposition, where Henry Adams discovers the implications of the dynamo. Edith helps Minnie Bourget do a French translation of Edith's "The Muses Tragedy," which appears in the July issue of the *Revue Hebdomadaire*, with an introductory note by Paul Bourget. Edith also visits her mother, who is bedridden. [Lewis 96–97; Benstock 113]
The Whartons tour for two weeks with the Bourgets through northwestern Italy and then return to Newport, but soon rent a cottage, The Poplars, in Lenox. [Lewis 97; Benstock 114]

August

"The Duchess at Prayer" [short story], *Scribner's Magazine*, 28: 153–60.
"The Rembrandt" [short story], *Hearst's International-Cosmopolitan*, 29: 429–37.
23 (Thu)   "Friends" [short story], *Youth's Companion*, 74: 405–06.
30   "Friends," *Youth's Companion*, 74: 417–18.

October

"The Line of Least Resistance" [short story], *Lippincott's Magazine*, 66: 559–70.
26 (Fri)   Writing to Edith Wharton, Henry James thanks her for sending him "the brilliant little tale," "The Line of Least Resistance." [*HJ Letters* 4: 170–71]

November

The Whartons return to Newport to close up Land's End, and then go to 884 Park Avenue, and an adjacent house, Number 882, which they have acquired for their servants. [Benstock 115]

1901

January

22 (Tue)   The death of Queen Victoria, who is succeeded by Edward VII.

February

"The Angel at the Grave" [short story], *Scribner's Magazine*, 29: 158–66.

"The Recovery" [short story], *Harper's Magazine*, 102: 468–77.

"More Love Letters of an Englishwoman" [parody], *Bookman*, 12: 562–63.

The Whartons go to Lenox for a week, negotiating for a land-purchase. [Lewis 100]

March

"The Moving Finger" [short story], *Harper's Magazine*, 102: 627–32.

12 (Tue)   Writing to Sara Norton, Edith tells her that negotiations for the purchase of a farm in Lenox have been concluded. [*Letters* 45]

April

6 (Sat)   *Crucial Instances* (New York: Scribner). It contains seven short stories: "The Duchess at Prayer," "The Angel at the Grave," "The Recovery," "Copy," "The Rembrandt," "The Moving Finger," and "The Confessional."
Crucial Instances (London: Murray).

May

21 (Mon)   Writing to Sara Norton, Edith tells her that Teddy is about to leave for New York and then England to see his ailing mother and bring her back to Lenox. Having no company, Edith therefore invites Sara to join her. [*Letters* 46]

June

Lucretia Jones dies in Paris, leaving a trust fund that came to be worth about $90,000 to Edith and outright bequests to Harry and Freddy, who are named as executors of her will. [Lewis 100–01]

29 (Sat)   Ownership of the Lenox property is conveyed to Edith for $40,600. Construction of The Mount soon begins. [Lewis 100]

July

The Whartons leave Boston on the *Commonwealth* for Liverpool. In London, where Freddy lives, Edith persuades him to give her more control over her trust fund. [Lewis 101]

August

"The Blashfields' 'Italian Cities' [review of Edwin H. and Evangeline W. Blashfield's *Italian Cities*]," *Bookman*, 13: 563–64. The Whartons go to Paris, where Harry lives, and Edith persuades him to do what Freddy had done. They also spend six days in Belgium, seeing Ghent, Antwerp, Bruges, and Brussels before returning in early September to Lenox. [Lewis 102; Benstock 121]

September

"Mould and Vase" [poem], *Atlantic Monthly*, 88: 343.

6 (Sun) President McKinley is shot by an assassin. He dies on the 14th and is succeeded by Theodore Roosevelt.

November

"Margaret of Cortona" [poem], *Harper's Magazine*, 103: 884–87.

1902

January

"Sub Umbra Liliorum: An Impression of Parma" [travel article], *Scribner's Magazine*, 31: 22–32.

24 (Fri) Writing to Sara Norton from 884 Park Avenue on her fortieth birthday, Edith thanks her for her note, which has "given me more pleasure than anything else the day is likely to bring," since "I excessively hate to be forty. . . . I'm not ready yet!" [*Letters* 55]

February

"Uses" [poem], *Scribner's Magazine*, 31: 180.

21 (Fri) *The Valley of Decision*, 2 vols. (New York: Scribner). It is dedicated to Paul and Minnie Bourget: "In Remembrance of Italian Days."

24 Writing to Sara Norton, whose father has helped her with books and advice while she was composing *The Valley of Decision*, Edith announces its publication and immanent arrival at "Shady Hill," their home in Cambridge. [*Letters*, 59]

March

"The Sanctuaries of the Pennine Alps" [travel article], *Scribner's Magazine*, 31: 353–64.

3 (Mon) Shortly after Teddy's departure for George Vanderbilt's estate, Biltmore, in North Carolina to recover from a bout of influenza, Edith has another breakdown. [Benstock 126]

Edith leaves for Washington, where she goes to the theatre and art galleries, sees Walter Berry and Bay Lodge, and gradually recovers. After ten days, during which Teddy joins her, she returns to New York. A significant period of critical and artistic activity ensued. [Lewis 105; Benstock 126; *Letters* 64]

April

"*Ulysses: A Drama*, by Stephen Phillips," *Bookman*, 15: 168–70.
The Valley of Decision (London: Murray).
The Whartons go to Boston and visit the Nortons in Cambridge and the Brooks Adamses in Quincy. [Benstock 127]

May

"*George Eliot*, by Leslie Stephen," *Bookman*, 15: 247–51.
The Whartons return to 884 Park Avenue. [*Letters* 61–63]

7 (Wed)   "The Theatres [Mrs. Fiske's performance in *Tess*]," *The Commercial Advertiser*, p. 9.
The English actress, Mrs. Patrick Campbell, asks Edith to translate Hermann Sudermann's play, *Es Lebe das Leben*, which she completes in September, and which appears the following month in New York as *The Joy of Living*. [Lewis 110]
The Whartons go to their rented home in Lenox. [Benstock 128]

31   The Boer War ends with the signing of the treaty of Vereeniging.

June

"The Quicksand" [short story], *Harper's Magazine*, 105: 13–21.
"Artemis to Actæon" [poem], *Scribner's Magazine*, 31: 661–62.

7 (Sat)   Writing to Sara Norton, Edith tells her that Lenox "has had its usual tonic effect on me." Mentioning that "everything is pushing up new shoots," she also speaks of the progress being made in building the new house, The Mount, and hopes to be living there in September. [*Letters* 66]

July

"The Three Francescas [essay on plays by Stephen Phillips, Gabriele d'Annunzio, and F. Marion Crawford]," *North American Review*, 175: 17–30.

August

"The Reckoning" [short story], *Harper's Magazine*, 105: 342–55.

"A Midsummer Week's Dream: August in Italy" [travel article],
Scribner's Magazine, 32: 212–22.

17 (Sun) Writing to Edith, Henry James tells her of having had an
advance copy of *The Wings of the Dove* sent to her and con-
gratulates her on her historical novel, *The Valley of Decision*,
as "a book so accomplished, pondered, saturated, so exquisitely
studied and so brilliant and interesting from a literary point
of view." But he also urges her to write on an American subject
(like New York) of the present: "the immediate, the real, the
ours, the yours, the novelist's that it waits for. . . . Profit,
be warned, by my awful example of exile and ignorance." [*HJ
Letters* 4: 234–36]

The Whartons go for a week to Newport to visit Winthrop
and Daisy Chanler for the christening of their son, Theodore,
named for President Roosevelt, who is also present and whose
company Edith enjoys. The Whartons also attend the finals
of the American tennis championship, about which Edith is
very enthusiastic, before returning to Lenox on the 28th.
[*Letters* 67; Benstock 129]

September

"The Bread of Angels" [poem], *Harper's Magazine*, 105: 583–85.

20 (Sat) The Whartons begin moving into The Mount. [*Letters* 72]

30 Writing to Sara Norton, Edith tells of having "enjoyed every
minute" of being in The Mount. "The views are exquisite, &
it is all so still & sylvan," and the lanes are purple with
Michaelmas daisies. [*Letters* 72–73]

October

Teddy has the first of a series of nervous collapses. [Lewis 111]

23 (Thu) The Whartons, Minnie Jones, Beatrix Jones, and Edith's secretary, Anna Bahlmann, attend the successful opening of *The
Joy of Living*, starring Mrs. Patrick Campbell, in New York with
her English theatre company. After a season in New York,
Mrs. Campbell takes it in 1903 to the midwest, the west coast,
and London. [Benstock 132–33]

Hermann Sudermann, *The Joy of Living (Es Lebe das Leben).
A Play in Five Acts* [translation] (New York: Scribner).

November

"The Lady's Maid's Bell" [short story], *Scribner's Magazine*, 32:
549–60.

"Vesalius in Zante" [poem], *North American Review*, 175:
625–31.

December

"The Mission of Jane" [short story], *Harper's Magazine*, 106: 63–74.

The Whartons visit the George Vanderbilts at their estate in North Carolina, Biltmore. [Lewis 114]

1903

January

1 (Thu) The Whartons attend the opening of Isabella Stewart Gardner's Fenway Court in Boston. [Lewis 115]

3 The Whartons leave Boston on the *Commonwealth* for Genoa, Edith's purpose being to write a series of articles on Italian villas and gardens that Richard Watson Gilder has requested for the *Century*. [*Letters* 73–74; Lewis 114, 116]

After arriving in Genoa, the Whartons go for three weeks to San Remo on the Italian Riviera. [Benstock 135]

February

"Mr. Paul on the Poetry of Matthew Arnold [review of Herbert W. Paul's *Matthew Arnold*]," *Lamp*, 26: 51–54.

"Picturesque Milan" [travel article], *Scribner's Magazine*, 33: 131–41.

The Whartons go to Rome. Edith explores the city but also drives out into the countryside, photographing villas and gardens, and taking notes on them. [Lewis 116–17]

March

10 (Tue) The Whartons leave Rome and visit Viterbo, Orvieto, Montefiascone, and "the delicious villas near Siena." [*Letters* 77, 80]

16 The Whartons arrive in Florence, where Violet Paget provides major assistance in helping Edith to see local villas. [*Letters* 80–81]

April

"A Torchbearer" [poem], *Scribner's Magazine*, 33: 504–05.

Hermann Sudermann, *The Joy of Living (Es Lebe das Leben). A Play in Five Acts* [translation] (London: Duckworth).

The Whartons go to Salsomaggiore, a mineral spa near Parma, where Edith has treatments for asthma, before going through the Veneto and Lombardy, and then spending ten days in Paris. [Lewis 119]

25 (Sat) The Whartons leave for America and go to Lenox. [Lewis 119]

June

5 (Fri) Writing to Sara Norton, Edith says: "My first few weeks in America are always miserable, because the tastes I am cursed with are all of a kind that cannot be gratified here. . . . I feel in America . . . out of sympathy with everything." She was also depressed by the results of a drought of nine weeks and a neglectful gardener. [*Letters* 84–85]

13 The Whartons sell Land's End for $122,500. [Lewis 122]

August

"Sanctuary" [novella], *Scribner's Magazine*, 34: 148–62.
Teddy has a nervous collapse and goes to stay with his brother, Billy, in Nahant. [Benstock 138–39]
Teddy joins Edith in Newport, where they visit Egerton Winthrop and also Mrs. George Vanderbilt at her home, The Breakers. [Lewis 123]

September

"Sanctuary," *Scribner's Magazine*, 34: 280–90.
The Whartons return to The Mount, where Teddy has another nervous collapse. [Lewis 123–24]

October

"Sanctuary," *Scribner's Magazine*, 34: 439–47.
"The Vice of Reading" [essay], *North American Review*, 177: 513–21.
The Whartons go to Newport for several weeks. [Lewis 124]

24 (Sat) *Sanctuary* (New York: Scribner).

November

"Sanctuary," *Scribner's Magazine*, 34: 570–80.
"Italian Villas and Their Gardens. Introduction: Italian Garden-Magic," *The Century Magazine*, 67: 21–24.
"Italian Villas and Their Gardens: Florentine Villas," *The Century Magazine*, 67: 25–33.
Sanctuary (London: Macmillan).

December

"The Dilettante" [short story], *Harper's Magazine*, 108: 139–43.
"Expiation" [short story], *Hearst's International-Cosmopolitan*, 36: 209–22.
"A Venetian Night's Entertainment" [short story], *Scribner's Magazine*, 34: 640–51.

"Italian Villas and Their Gardens: Sienese Villas," *The Century Magazine*, 67: 162–64.

2 (Wed)   The Whartons leave from New York on the *Cedric* for England, where they spend ten days in London. [Lewis 124,128; Benstock 139]

Henry James comes up to London from Lamb House to meet Edith. He and the Whartons have lunch and spend the afternoon together. [Lewis 124]

1904

January

The Whartons go to Paris, where they buy a motor car. After visiting the Bourgets at their home in Costebelle, they drive to Grasse and Cannes, where they are stormbound for a week. [Lewis 128–29]

February

13 (Sat)   "The Other Two" [short story], *Collier's*, 32: 15–17, 20.

"Italian Villas and Their Gardens: Roman Villas," *The Century Magazine*, 67: 562–64, 566, 568–72.

The Whartons drive to Monte Carlo, then to Genoa, where bad weather sends them back to Monte Carlo. [Lewis 129]

March

"The Descent of Man" [short story], *Scribner's Magazine*, 35: 313–22.

After Edith has recovered from nervous indigestion, headaches, influenza, and laryngitis, the Whartons leave Monte Carlo and drive west through southern France. [Lewis 129; *Letters* 89]

April

"The Letter" [short story], *Harper's Magazine*, 108: 781–89.

"Italian Villas and Their Gardens: Villas Near Rome," *The Century Magazine*, 67: 860–61, 863–64, 868, 870–74.

The Whartons drive to Pau near the Spanish border and then turn north, going to Périgueux, Limoges, Bourges, Blois, and Paris, after which they return to London by late April. [Lewis 129–30]

30 (Sat)   *The Descent of Man and Other Stories* (New York: Scribner), dedicated to Edward L. Burlingame, "My First and Kindest Critic." It contains nine short stories: "The Descent of Man," "The Mission of Jane," "The Other Two," "The Quicksand," "The Dilettante," "The Reckoning," "Expiation," "The Lady's Maid's Bell," and "A Venetian Night's Entertainment."

The Descent of Man And Other Stories (London: Macmillan). It also contains "The Letter."

May

The Whartons make various motor trips in England, including a visit to Henry James at Lamb House in Rye. [Lewis 130]

June

The Whartons sell their vehicle to avoid significant import duty and return to Lenox. They then buy an American motor car. [Lewis 130–31, 136]

25 (Mon) Writing to William Crary Brownell, Edith thanks him for reviews of *The Descent of Man*, but rejects "the continued cry that I am an echo of Mr. James (whose books of the last ten years I can't read, much as I delight in the man)." [*Letters* 91]

July

The Wharton's summer entertainment season begins with visits from Daisy Chanler, Bay and Bessie Lodge, Egerton Winthrop, and Walter Berry, who stays for some weeks. [Benstock 142]

August

"The House of the Dead Hand" [short story], *Atlantic Monthly*, 94: 145–60.
"The Last Asset" [short story], *Scribner's Magazine*, 36: 150–68.
"Italian Villas and Their Gardens: Lombard Villas," *The Century Magazine*, 68: 541–54.
Touring through New England with Walter Berry, Edith meets Gaillard Lapsley, an American teaching at Trinity College, Cambridge University, who will become a close friend. [Lewis 137]

September

Edith's brother, Harry, comes from Paris for a visit at The Mount. [Benstock 143]
Edith and Walter Berry drive to Ashfield, Massachusetts, to see the Charles Eliot Norton family at their summer home, about forty miles from The Mount. [Lewis 138]

October

"Italian Villas and Their Gardens: Villas of Venetia," *The Century Magazine*, 68: 885–95.
"Italian Villas and Their Gardens: Genoese Villas," *The Century Magazine*, 68: 895–902.

Henry James and Howard Sturgis join Walter Berry as guests at The Mount. James speaks of it as "this elegant, this wonderful abode," and calls it "an exquisite and marvellous place, a delicate French chateau mirrored in a Massachusetts pond . . ., and a monument to the almost too impeccable taste of its so accomplished mistress." He also acknowledges that under the influence of Edith Wharton, he has "been won over to motoring, for which the region is . . . delightful." [*HJ Letters* 4: 325, 330]

November

2 (Wed)   *Italian Villas and Their Gardens*, illus. Maxfield Parrish (New York: Century). It is dedicated to Vernon Lee: "Who, Better Than Anyone Else Has Understood And Interpreted The Garden-Magic Of Italy."
Italian Villas And Their Gardens, illus. Maxfield Parrish (London: John Lane, The Bodley Head).

18   Writing to Edith, Henry James sends her a copy of *The Golden Bowl*. [*HJ Letters* 4: 334]

December

"The Pot-Boiler" [short story], *Scribner's Magazine*, 36: 696–712. The Whartons return to New York. [Lewis 142]

1905

January

"The House of Mirth" [novel], *Scribner's Magazine*, 37: 33–43.
2 (Mon)   Henry James arrives at 884 Park Ave. to visit the Whartons. [Lewis 143]

February

"The House of Mirth," *Scribner's Magazine*, 37: 143–57.

March

"The House of Mirth," *Scribner's Magazine*, 37: 319–37.
The Whartons visit friends in Washington. [Lewis 144]
16 (Thu)   The Whartons dine at the White House, Edith being seated at President Theodore Roosevelt's right hand. He becomes a friend for whom she was to write a memorial poem. [Lewis 144–45]

April

"The House of Mirth," *Scribner's Magazine*, 37: 469–86.
Edith goes from New York to Paris with her housekeeper-companion, Catharine Gross. [Lewis 146]

Italian Backgrounds [travel sketches], illus. E. C. Peixotto (New York: Scribner).
Italian Backgrounds (London: Macmillan).

May

"The House of Mirth," *Scribner's Magazine*, 37: 549–64.
"Mr. Sturgis's '*Belchamber*,' " *Bookman*, 21: 307–10.
Edith, suffering from asthma, goes with Catharine Gross, her housekeeper-companion, to Salsomaggiore for a health cure. Then, after a few more days in Paris, they return to Lenox, where, during the summer, Edith entertains many guests, including Henry James, Walter Berry, Sara Norton, Bay Lodge, and Egerton Winthrop. [Lewis 146–47]

June

"The House of Mirth," *Scribner's Magazine*, 37: 738–53.
Henry James makes a brief visit to The Mount, and Edith drives with him to Charles Eliot Norton's summer home at Ashfield. [Lewis 146]

July

"The House of Mirth," *Scribner's Magazine*, 38: 81–100.
The Whartons and Bay Lodge drive to South Berwick, Maine, the home of Sarah Orne Jewett. [Lewis 150]

August

"The House of Mirth," *Scribner's Magazine*, 38: 210–20.
The Whartons and the Walter Maynards drive along the Connecticut River and lunch in Cornish, New Hampshire, with Maxfield Parrish, who had illustrated *Italian Villas and Their Gardens*, and meet the American novelist, Winston Churchill. [Lewis 150]

September

"The House of Mirth," *Scribner's Magazine*, 38: 332–49.
"Maurice Hewlett's '*The Fool Errant*,' " *Bookman*, 22: 64–67.
2 (Sat)   "The Best Man" [short story], *Collier's*, 35: 14–17, 21–22.

October

"The House of Mirth," *Scribner's Magazine*, 38: 445–62.
14 (Sat)   *The House of Mirth*, illus. A. B. Wenzell (New York: Scribner). By the end of the year it has become the best-selling novel in the country. [Lewis 151]
16   *The House of Mirth* (London: Macmillan).

November

"The House of Mirth," *Scribner's Magazine*, 38: 605–17.

8 (Wed) Writing to Edith, Henry James tells her of having just read the final serial installment of *The House of Mirth*, and says: "I very much admire that fiction, . . . finding it carried off with a high, strong hand and an admirable touch, finding it altogether a superior thing." [*HJ Letters* 4: 373–74]

11 Writing to Charles Scribner, Edith thanks him for the news that 80,000 copies of *The House of Mirth* have been sold and that many thousands more are being printed. She also tells him that she has plans for dramatizing the novel, "as I am having so many bids for it." [*Letters* 95–96]

December

"The Introducers" [short story], *Ainslee's*, 16: 139–48.

18 (Mon) The Whartons leave The Mount for Washington, where they stay briefly before going to Biltmore for Christmas with the George Vanderbilts. They then go to New York. [Lewis 159]

1906

January

"The Introducers," *Ainslee's*, 16: 61–67.

Clyde Fitch calls on Edith proposing to collaborate with her on a dramatization of *The House of Mirth*. They agree that he will provide the scenario and she will write the dialogue. They then sign a contract with the producer, Charles Frohman. [Lewis 171; *Letters* 103–04]

February

"The Hermit and the Wild Woman" [short story], *Scribner's Magazine*, 39: 145–56.

21 (Wed) Writing to Sara Norton, Edith thanks her for William Ostwald's recently published lecture, *Individuality and Immortality*, and comments on "how it lifts one up to hear such a voice as that in the midst of all the psychological-pietistical juggling of which your friend W. James is the source & chief distributor!" [*Letters* 101–02]

March

17 (Sat) The Whartons leave New York on the *Philadelphia* and arrive on the 25th in Paris, where they stay at the Hotel Domenici. [Lewis 161]

Paul Bourget introduces Edith to friends in the intellectual and social circles of Paris, notably the Comtesse Charlotte de Cossé-Brissac, the Comtesse Anna de Noailles, and Charles du Bos, who will translate *The House of Mirth*. [Lewis 161–62]

April

"In Trust" [short story], *Appleton's Booklover's Magazine*, 7: 432–40.
The Whartons move into the town-house of Edith's brother, Harry, at 3 Place des Etats-Unis. [Lewis 165]
Teddy goes to buy a car in England, where Edith joins him on the 25th. [Lewis 165]

26 (Thu) The Whartons begin their first motor tour in England, going to the Isle of Wight, Salisbury, and Bath, where they are briefly joined by Henry James. Afterwards they drive to Stratford-on-Avon and Cambridge, where they see Gaillard Lapsley. [Lewis 165–66]

May

Henry James joins them for a visit to Howard Sturgis's home, Queen's Acre, near Windsor, where they meet Percy Lubbock. [Lewis 167]
After returning to Paris, the Whartons go on a two-week motor tour with her brother, Harry, which leads to a series of travel articles for the *Atlantic* that are later gathered into *A Motor-Flight Through France*. They visit Amiens, Beauvais, Rouen, Fontainebleau, Orléans, Tours, Châteauroux, George Sand's home at Nohant, and Clermont-Ferrand, before driving back to Paris. [Lewis 168–69]

June

The Whartons return to Lenox. [Lewis 170]

August

"Madame de Treymes" [novella], *Scribner's Magazine*, 40: 167–92.
Edith and Clyde Fitch complete the dramatic version of *The House of Mirth*, and rehearsals begin. [Lewis 172]

September

14 (Fri) The Whartons and Walter Berry go to Detroit for the opening of the dramatic version of *The House of Mirth*, which is successful. [Lewis 172]

October

22 (Mon)   The dramatic version of *The House of Mirth* opens at the Savoy Theatre in New York City, but runs for only a few days. [Lewis 172; *Letters* 110]

December

"A Motor-Flight Through France" [travel serial], *Atlantic Monthly*, 98: 733–41.

1907

January

"A Motor-Flight Through France," *Atlantic Monthly*, 99: 98–105.
"The Fruit of the Tree" [novel], *Scribner's Magazine*, 41: 10–23.

4 (Fri)   The Whartons leave New York for France on the *Amerika*, and in Paris stay in an apartment at 58 Rue de Varenne, in the Faubourg St. Germain, that they have rented from the George Vanderbilts. [Lewis 173; Benstock 156]
Edith meets Morton Fullerton, a former student of Charles Eliot Norton's, a friend of the Norton family, and Paris correspondent of the London *Times*. [Lewis 183; Benstock 169]

February

"A Motor-Flight Through France," *Atlantic Monthly*, 99: 242–46.
"The Fruit of the Tree," *Scribner's Magazine*, 41: 153–66.

March

"The Fruit of the Tree," *Scribner's Magazine*, 41: 269–83.

2 (Sat)   *Madame de Treymes*, illus. Alonzo Kimball (New York: Scribner).
Madame de Treymes (London: Macmillan).

7   Henry James arrives in Paris, where he stays with the Whartons in their apartment at 58 Rue de Varenne. [*HJ Letters* 4: 459]

20   The Whartons leave Paris on their second motor-tour of France, this time with Henry James. They visit Châteauroux, Nohant, Poitiers, Pau, St. Jean-de-Luz, Lourdes, Cauterets, Toulouse, Albi, Carcasonne, Nîmes, Aix, Hyères, Avignon, Lyons, Dijon, Auxerre, Sens, and Paris. [*HJ Letters* 4: 459; Lewis 177–79]

April

"The Fruit of the Tree," *Scribner's Magazine*, 41: 414–28.

13 (Sat)   Writing to Howard Sturgis, James tells of having returned to Paris on the previous evening after "a wondrous, miraculous

motor-tour of three weeks and a day." He characterizes the trip as an occasion of "really *seeing* this large incomparable France in our friend's chariot of fire," and calls it "almost the time of my life." [*HJ Letters* 4: 442–43]

21   Writing to Sara Norton, Edith tells her that shortly after she returned to Paris, Gaillard Lapsley proposed a little motor trip near Paris, and so she, Lapsley, and Henry James drove through Burgundy, visiting Avallon, Vézelay, and Auxerre. She also mentions frequently seeing Morton Fullerton, whom she calls "very intelligent, but slightly mysterious." [*Letters* 112–14]

May

"The Fruit of the Tree," *Scribner's Magazine*, 41: 620–34.

15 (Wed)   Writing to Charles Eliot Norton, Edith tells him that Henry James has left after a mutually enjoyable two-month stay with the Whartons: "The more one knows him the more one wonders & admires the mixture of wisdom & tolerance, of sensitiveness & sympathy, that makes his heart even more interesting to contemplate than his mind." [*Letters* 114–15]

June

"The Fruit of the Tree," *Scribner's Magazine*, 41: 717–34.
The Whartons leave for America on the *Adriatic* and then go to Lenox. [Lewis 179; *Letters* 114–15]

July

"The Fruit of the Tree," *Scribner's Magazine*, 42: 89–112.

August

"The Fruit of the Tree," *Scribner's Magazine*, 42: 197–216.

September

"The Fruit of the Tree," *Scribner's Magazine*, 42: 357–78.

October

"The Fruit of the Tree," *Scribner's Magazine*, 42: 447–68.

19 (Sat)   *The Fruit of the Tree*, illus. Alonzo Kimball (New York: Scribner).
The Fruit of the Tree (London: Macmillan).
Morton Fullerton, now on a visit to America, comes to The Mount bringing a letter from Henry James, and stays for several days, leaving on the 26th. [Lewis 183–84]

29   Edith begins a private journal addressed to Fullerton. [Lewis 184]

November

"The Fruit of the Tree," *Scribner's Magazine*, 42: 595–613.

"The Sonnets of Eugene Lee-Hamilton [review of Eugene Lee-Hamilton's *The Sonnets of the Wingless Hours*],"*Bookman*, 26: 251–53.

December

5 (Thu)   The Whartons go to France and stay again at 58 Rue de Varenne, where Teddy has a nervous depression but Edith soon leads a busy social life, and sees a good deal of Morton Fullerton, who has returned to Paris. [Lewis 191–95]

1908

January

"The Old Pole Star" [poem], *Scribner's Magazine*, 43: 68.

"A Second Motor-Flight Through France" [travel serial], *Atlantic Monthly*, 101: 3–9.

13 (Mon)   Edith and Morton Fullerton attend a performance of Gabriele D'Annunzio's love tragedy, *La Figlia di Iorio*, and in her diary she characterizes the time spent in their theatre box as "unforgettable hours." Between 1 January and 29 February, she sees Fullerton twenty four times. [*Letters* 127–28; Benstock 179]

February

"A Second Motor-Flight Through France," *Atlantic Monthly*, 101: 167–73.

12 (Wed)   Teddy goes to visit Ralph Curtis, a painter and art collector, and his wife, Lise, at their villa at Beaulieu, near Monte Carlo. [Lewis 193,203]

15   Edith and Morton Fullerton have an especially memorable day as they drive through St. Germain-en-Laye and Conflans on the way to Herblay, home of the unconventional early nineteenth century novelist and erotically candid letter-writer, Hortense Allart. Writing in her diary that evening, Edith expressed a feeling of intimate togetherness with him. [Lewis 204]

21   Teddy returns from the Riviera. [Lewis 207]

March

"A Second Motor-Flight Through France," *Atlantic Monthly*, 101: 345–52.

16 (Mon)   Writing to Sara Norton, Edith tells her "I enjoy Paris more & more, as I get hold of more agreeable & interesting people." [*Letters* 136]

21   Teddy, suffering from gout, leaves for New York on the *Philadelphia*, and goes to Hot Springs, Arkansas, for treatment. Edith continues to see a good deal of Fullerton, and grows closer and closer to him. [Lewis 209]

April

"A Second Motor-Flight Through France," *Atlantic Monthly*, 101: 474–82.

13 (Mon)   Edith moves to the residence at 3 Place des Etats-Unis of her brother, Harry, who has gone to America. She soon meets the painter, Jacques-Emile Blanche. [*Letters* 139–40; Lewis 210, 212]

24   Henry James arrives in Paris for a two-week visit with Edith, who persuades him to sit for his portrait by Blanche. [*HJ Letters* 4: 491]

May

Edith decides to begin an intimate relationship with Fullerton, hoping to go off with him to "a little inn in the country in the depths of a green wood," but they do not seem to have been able to make the arrangements. She does show him her love diary, however, as she is about to leave for America. [Benstock 184–85]

23 (Sat)   Edith leaves Paris for Le Havre and travels on the *Provence* to New York, where Teddy meets her and goes with her to Lenox. [Lewis 227–28]

June

"The Verdict" [short story], *Scribner's Magazine*, 43: 689–93.

11 (Thu)   Writing to Morton Fullerton, with whom she is carrying on an active correspondence, Edith calls him "my adored, my own love, you who have given me the only moments of real life I have ever known." [Lewis 229]

Walter Berry visits Edith at The Mount. [Lewis 231]

July

"Moonrise Over Tyringham" [poem], *The Century Magazine*, 76: 356–57.

1 (Wed)   Writing to Morton Fullerton, Edith thanks him for breaking his "silence of nineteen days" with a letter she has just received after sending him a cable, and asks for "a line once a week," hoping that the dwindling of his correspondence doesn't mean the fading of his affection. [*Letters* 156–58]

Edith recovers from six weeks of hay fever. [Lewis 232]

August
      "The Pretext" [short story], *Scribner's Magazine*, 44: 173–87.
26 (Wed) Writing to Morton Fullerton, Edith expresses bewilderment at his failure to respond to her letters during the past month: "this incomprehensible silence, the sense of your utter indifference to everything that concerns me, has stunned me." She tells him that "This is the last time I shall write you, dear, unless the strange spell is broken." [*Letters* 161–62]

September
26 (Sat) *The Hermit and the Wild Woman and Other Stories* (New York: Scribner). It contains sevem short stories: "The Hermit and the Wild Woman," "The Last Asset," "In Trust," "The Pretext," "The Verdict," "The Pot-Boiler," and "The Best Man."
      The Hermit and the Wild Woman and Other Stories (London: Macmillan).

October
      "Les Metteurs en Scène" [short story], *Revue des Deux Mondes*, 67: 692–708.
      "Life" [poem], *Atlantic Monthly*, 102: 501–04.
10 (Sat) *A Motor-Flight Through France* (New York: Scribner).
      A Motor-Flight Through France (London: Macmillan).
13   Writing to Edith, Henry James tells her of being "deeply distressed at the situation you describe:" her involvement with Morton Fullerton, who has a history of promiscuous behavior. James tells her that he does not "pretend to understand or to imagine." Instead, he simply urges her to "sit tight yourself *and go through the movements of life*. That keeps up our connection with life – I mean of the immediate and apparent life; behind which, all the while, the deeper and darker and the unapparent, in which things *really* happen to us, learns, under that hygiene, to stay in its place." [*HJ Letters* 4: 494–95]
21   Charles Eliot Norton dies. In her last letter to him, Edith had sent him her love and her gratitude at being "one of the many who have been stimulated & delighted by your interest and sympathy, & helped by your affection." [*Letters* 163–64]
30   Edith leaves for Europe on the *Provence* with Walter Berry as a fellow passenger. Teddy remains in New York. [Lewis 239; Benstock 192]

November
      "The Choice" [short story], *The Century Magazine*, 77: 32–40.
      After a two night stay in Paris, where Edith sees Morton Fullerton, she and Berry go to England, where they see

Henry James, Howard Sturgis, and Gaillard Lapsley before Berry leaves for Cairo, where he has been appointed a judge on the International Tribunal. [Lewis 239–40; Benstock 192]

16 (Mon)   On a drive with Henry James from Lamb House to Queen's Acre, James suggests a detour to Box Hill, where he introduces Edith to George Meredith, who interrupts his reading of *A Motor-Flight Through France*, and warmly receives them. [Lewis 240; *Glance* 250–54]

After Queen's Acre, Edith goes to London, staying with Lady St. Helier at 52 Portland Place, and meeting many socialites and also literary figures like James Barrie, Edmund Gosse, Max Beerbohm, Thomas Hardy, and John Galsworthy. [Lewis 242]

28   Edith goes for a weekend to Cliveden, the country home of William Waldorf Astor and his wife, Nancy. [*Letters* 167; Lewis 242]

December

Edith goes for a weekend party in her honor given by Lord and Lady Elcho at Stanway, their country home in the Cotswolds. There Edith meets two young Englishmen who will be close friends, Robert Norton and John Hugh Smith. [Lewis 242–44]

19 (Sat)   Writing fom Portland Place to Morton Fullerton, Edith addresses him as "Mr. Fullerton" and asks for the return of her letters to him. Telling him that she will be in Paris for a day only, on the 21st, she asks that he send them by registered mail to her on that day at her brother Harry's home in the Place des Etats Unis. Fullerton did not do so, but sent a message saying that his feelings for her have survived. [*Letters* 170; Benstock 193]

19   Howard Sturgis, his nephew, William Haynes-Smith, and Edith leave London in her motorcar and go to Rye, where they stay with Henry James at Lamb House. [Benstock 196]

21   Sturgis, Haynes-Smith, and Edith go to Paris and then take a week's drive to Dijon and Avignon before returning to Paris, where they celebrate New Year's Eve at the Café de Paris and at 58 Rue de Varenne. [Lewis 250; Benstock 196–97]

1909

January

"All Souls' " [poem], *Scribner's Magazine*, 45: 22–23.

18 (Mon)   Teddy arrives from New York, suffering from insomnia, bodily pain, and depression. [Lewis 251–52]

February

12 (Fri)   Writing to John Hugh Smith, Edith says: "I wonder, among all the tangles of this mortal coil, which one contains tighter knots to undo, & consequently suggests more tugging, & pain, & diversified elements of misery, than the marriage tie." [*Letters* 175]

23   Writing to Morton Fullerton, Edith asks him to come and dine "with the old friend . . . qui t'aime, qui t'aime, mais qui sait qu'elle ne sait pas te le dire, et qui se taira désormais [who loves you, who loves you, but who knows that she doesn't know how to tell you, and who will henceforth keep silent]." [*Letters* 176]

The Whartons motor for ten days through southern France. On their return to Paris Teddy begins massage and electrical treatment. [Lewis 253]

March

"The Bolted Door" [short story], *Scribner's Magazine*, 45: 288–308.

April

ca. 15   Teddy leaves for the United States and The Mount, and Edith renews her relationship with Fullerton. [Lewis 255–56]

17 (Sat)   *Artemis to Actæon and Other Verse* (New York: Scribner). It contains 25 poems: "Artemus to Actæon," "Life," "Vesalius in Zante," "Margaret of Cortona," "A Torchbearer," "The Mortal Lease," "Experience," "Grief," "Chartres," "Two Backgrounds," "The Tomb of Ilaria Giunigi," "The One Grief," "The Eumenides," "Orpheus," "An Autumn Sunset," "Moonrise Over Tyringham," "All Souls," "All Saints," "The Old Pole Star," "A Grave," "Non Dolet," "A Hunting-Song," "Survival," "Uses," and "A Meeting."

Artemis to Actæon and Other Verse (London: Macmillan).

The lease on 58 Rue la Varenne expires and Edith moves to the Hotel Crillon. [Lewis 257]

May

Edith gives Morton Fullerton a copy of her poem "Ogrin the Hermit," which she has dedicated to him, telling him that through the experience of loving they will always be connected, and she asks him to read it aloud to her. [Lewis 256]

Writing to Morton Fullerton, Edith thanks him for his response to "Ogrin the Hermit," and asks him to go back with her "gaily & goodhumouredly to our former state." [*Letters* 179–80]

June

"His Father's Son" [short story], *Scribner's Magazine*, 45: 657–65.

"A Grave" [poem], *Current Literature*, 46: 685.

3 (Thu)   Edith and Fullerton go to Folkestone, England, prior to his trip to the United States to see his parents. On the following day they go to London, take Suite 92 at the Charing Cross Hotel, and spend the night together engaging in sexual relations, an experience that Edith captures in her poem, "Terminus." [Lewis 258–60]

5   Fullerton leaves for America, and Edith and Henry James drive to Queen's Acre. Afterwards she goes to London, again visiting Lady St. Helier, and then drives to Oxford to see Percy Lubbock and to Cambridge to see Gaillard Lapsley, and revisits Queen's Acre and Lamb House until Fullerton returns. [Lewis 260–61]

July

"The Daunt Diana" [short story], *Scribner's Magazine*, 46: 35–41.

Fullerton returns to England from the United States. [Lewis 262]

16 (Fri)   Writing to Howard Sturgis, Henry James tells him that Edith and Fullerton arrived in Rye on the 12th and that she whirled him in her motor-car through Sussex, parting from him in Canterbury on the previous afternoon. Calling her "the Fire-Bird," from the Diaghilev ballet set to Stravinsky's music, he says: "So she set the piper piping hard – and I danced till my aged legs would no more – and (the worst is) it was all beautiful and interesting and damnable." [*HJ Letters* 4: 526–27]

Edith and Fullerton leave England for Paris. [Lewis 260, 262; *Letters* 188]

Edith takes an unfurnished apartment at 53 Rue de Varenne. [Lewis 258; *Letters* 185]

August

"The Debt" [short story], *Scribner's Magazine*, 46: 165–72.

12 (Thu)   Writing to Fullerton, Edith evokes being with him at Lamb House a month previous, and says: "During that month I have been completely happy. I have had everything in life that I ever longed for, & more than I ever imagined." [*Letters* 189]

15   Walter Berry stops in Paris on his way to the United States, taking a vacation from his judicial position in Cairo. [Benstock 220]

17	Teddy's mother, Nancy Spring Wharton, dies in her home at Lenox, leaving Teddy about $67,000 and some land. [Lewis 267, 277]
20	Writing to Sara Norton, Edith tells her of having seen on the 18th her first airplane flight: "It sailed obliquely across the Place [de la Concorde], incredibly high above the obelisk, against a golden sunset, with a new moon between flitting clouds, & crossing the Seine in the direction of the Panthéon, lost itself in a flight of birds that was just crossing the sky, reappeared far off, a speck against the clouds, & disappeared at last into the twilight. And it was the Comte de Lambert . . . & it was the *first time* that an aeroplane has ever crossed a great city!!" [*Letters* 191–92]
21	Bay Lodge dies from a heart attack. His father, Senator Henry Cabot Lodge, asks Edith to write a memorial, which was published in February 1910, in which she said: "he, who had so many gifts, had above all, the gift of life." [Benstock 221]

September

30 (Thu)	Henry Adams arranges a dinner at Voisin's bringing together Edith and Bernard Berenson, who is to become a close friend. [Lewis 268–70]

October

"Full Circle" [short story], *Scribner's Magazine*, 46: 408–19.

November

Teddy arrives in Paris with his sister, Nannie. At first he is very cheerful, but then he becomes severely depressed. [Lewis 272, 274]

Teddy drives Nannie to Pau in southwestern France, where she is to vacation, and then returns to Paris. Meanwhile, Edith and her secretary, Anna Bahlmann, who has recently come from America, go for a week to Germany. [Lewis 275]

December

"Ogrin the Hermit" [poem], *Atlantic Monthly*, 104: 844–48.

2 (Thu)	Writing to Sara Norton from Munich, Edith tells her how much she and Anna have been enjoying Munich's museums and theatre, and that they leave the following day for Würzburg and Karlsruhe on the trip back to Paris. She also says that Teddy is not at all well, but that Nannie refuses to recognize his nervous disorder. [*Letters* 193–95]

8	Teddy and Edith return to the Hotel Crillon, and Teddy tells her that during the previous summer he had embezzled money from Edith's trust funds, bought an apartment in Boston, and lived there with a mistress. It gradually becomes apparent that he had embezzled at least $50,000. In response, his brother, William, eventually transfers $50,000 from Teddy's inheritance to a trust fund of Edith's. [Lewis 275, 277]
13 (Mon)	Writing to Edith (now "Dearest Edith") in response to her recent letter from Germany, Henry James tells her of having "deeply revelled" in her descriptions, especially of "dear old rococo Munich." [*HJ Letters* 4: 537–38]
	Teddy goes to Boston. [Lewis 276]

1910

January

	"Afterward" [short story], *The Century Magazine*, 79: 321–39.
3 (Mon)	Edith moves from the Hotel Crillon to 53 Rue de Varenne just prior to the selling of the New York houses, from which she will transfer furniture. [Lewis 278; Benstock 229]

February

	"George Cabot Lodge" [article], *Scribner's Magazine*, 47: 236–39.

March

	"The Legend" [short story], *Scribner's Magazine*, 47: 278–91.
	Teddy arrives in Paris, and exhibits manic-depressive behavior, especially the latter. Nerve doctors are unable to treat him successfully and his mental ill-health makes Edith very unhappy. [Lewis 281–83]
17 (Thu)	Edith goes to London to see Henry James, who has come for medical examination. Teddy is being looked after by Nannie in Paris. [*Letters* 199–200; Benstock 233]
18	Writing to Fullerton, Edith tells of first seeing James: "we fell on each other's necks & stood tranced in long embraces; and he was *so* glad to see me that I understood quite well why I had got up at 6:30 a.m. to come to him!" [*Letters* 199–200]
19	Writing to Fullerton, Edith tells of her plan to spend time at Lamb House with James, who is suffering from nervous depression, and to have Teddy come to Folkestone for a fortnight while she shuttles between them. [*Letters* 201–04]
25	Teddy joins her at Folkestone. They return to Paris in early April. [*Letters* 205; Lewis 283]

April

25 (Mon)   Edith gives a tea-party at 53 Rue de Varenne for Theodore Roosevelt, who is on a tour of Africa and Europe. [*Letters* 211]

May

Edith takes Teddy to Lausanne to see a neurologist. [Benstock 237]

6 (Fri)   The death of Edward VII, who is succeeded by George V.

June

"The Eyes" [short story], *Scribner's Magazine*, 47: 671–80.

Teddy goes to a Swiss sanitorium near Konstanz, and is treated with massage, hydrotherapy, and electrotherapy. [Lewis 284]

20 (Mon)   Walter Berry resigns from the International Tribune at Cairo and comes to Paris. [Lewis 285]

July

Berry is given a guest suite in the Wharton's apartment, where he remains for almost six months. Edith's relationship with Fullerton remains affectionate but becomes less intense. [Lewis 285,287]

Edith considers Teddy's condition a "nervous breakdown" and decides that he shall no longer manage her money affairs and household matters. She agrees, however, with his proposal that he take a long trip to the American West after leaving the sanitorium, suggests that their American and Parisian friend, Johnson Morton, accompany him, and offers him a motor car. [Lewis 289]

14 (Thu)   Edith leaves Paris for Nancy, Dijon, and Divonne les Bains, apparently with her secretary, Anna Bahlmann, on a short trip. [*Letters* 220–21]

Teddy leaves the sanitorium and goes to Bern for medical consultation before returning to Paris. [Lewis 290–91]

August

"The Letters" [short story], *The Century Magazine*, 80: 485–92. Edith makes a brief trip to England and Lamb House. [Lewis 290]

5 (Fri)   Edith, whom James calls the "Firebird," and "the devastating angel," takes James in her motor car to visit Howard Sturgis at Queen's Acre, Windsor. [*HJ Letters* 4: 558]

12   James and his ailing brother, William, who has been visiting him, leave for the United States, where William is to die two weeks later. [Benstock 240]

Edith and Teddy go south to the Cote-d'Or and then to a
hotel in a former Carthusian monastery near Mont Blanc.
[Lewis 291–92]

September

"The Blond Beast" [short story], *Scribner's Magazine*, 48:
291–304.

"The Letters," *The Century Magazine*, 80: 641–50.

Edith and Teddy go to the United States, staying at the
Belmont Hotel at Park Avenue and 41st St. in New York City,
as preparations are made for Teddy to be taken not just to the
American West but round the world by their friend, Johnson
Morton. [Lewis 292; Benstock 240]

October

"The Letters," *The Century Magazine*, 80: 812–19.

16 (Sun)   Teddy and Johnson Morton leave for California. [Lewis 292]

17   Edith has dinner with three of her closest male friends, all
of whom are visiting the United States: Henry James, Morton
Fullerton, and Walter Berry. [Lewis 292–93]

18   Edith leaves for Europe on the *Prinzessin Cécilie*, arriving
in Cherbourg and Paris on the 24th. [Lewis 292–93; *Letters*
223–25]

22   *Tales of Men and Ghosts* (New York: Scribner). It contains
ten short stories: "The Bolted Door," "His Father's Son," "The
Daunt Diana," "The Debt," "Full Circle," "The Legend," "The
Eyes," "The Blond Beast," "Afterward," and "The Letters."
Tales of Men and Ghosts (London: Macmillan).

November

22 (Tue)   Teddy and Morton leave California for the Far East. [Lewis 294]

December

"The Comrade" [poem], *Atlantic Monthly*, 106: 785–87.

Walter Berry moves from the Wharton guest suite to a nearby
apartment in the Rue St. Guillaume. [Lewis 285, 295]

1911

January

4 (Wed)   Writing to Bernard Berenson, Edith tells of working on *Ethan
Frome* and having very little of a social life, "because I can't
when I'm story-telling." She sees few people other than Walter
Berry, Morton Fullerton, and Paul Bourget. [*Letters* 232–33;
Lewis 295]

March

"Summer Afternoon (Bodiam Castle, Sussex)" [poem], *Scribner's Magazine*, 49: 277–78.

5 (Sun)   Writing to Barrett Wendell, a professor of English at Harvard, Edith tells him of having been in touch with William Dean Howells in America and Edmund Gosse in England as part of an effort to secure the Nobel Prize for Henry James. [*Letters* 234–35]

April

6 (Thu)   Teddy lands at Marseilles and goes to Paris. He begs and then demands that he be given back control over her financial affairs, and subsequently reverses himself and admits that he is not well enough to do so. [Lewis 300]

Teddy leaves for the United States and goes to Boston for medical treatment. [Lewis 301]

May

10 (Wed)   Suffering from hay fever, Edith goes to Milan and Salsomaggiore for treatment. While at Salsomaggiore, Edith receives a letter from her American financial and legal advisor, Herman Edgar, telling her that Teddy is seeking to regain control over her finances. Edith is offended at Teddy's breach of their agreement, insists that it be honored, and asks that Teddy be removed as a trustee of her estate. [Lewis 301; *Letters* 236].

27   Edith leaves Salsomaggiore for Paris. [*Letters* 240]

June

24 (Sat)   Edith leaves on the *Philadelphia* for New York and arrives at The Mount on 2 July. [Lewis 302; *Letters* 242]

July

"Other Times, Other Manners" [short story], *The Century Magazine*, 82: 344–52.

8 (Sat)   A group of close friends gathers at The Mount, all visiting from England: Henry James, Gaillard Lapsley, and John Hugh Smith. [Lewis 302]

12   Smith leaves, as does Lapsley on the 13th. Soon after, James and Edith are joined by Teddy, whose moods range from harsh abusiveness about money matters to fits of weeping and apology. Before James leaves, he advises Edith to sell The Mount and separate from Teddy. [Lewis 303–04]

14   James leaves. For the next ten days Teddy's abusive behavior continues and Edith comes to consider leaving him. [Lewis 304]

22   Writing to Teddy's lawyer brother, William Fisher Wharton, Edith summarizes Teddy's behavior and explains that he has accepted her offer to give him the management of The Mount and to make monthly cash deposits for that purpose. He has also agreed to give up his trusteeship. When she shows Teddy the letter, however, he angrily rejects its terms and proposes that they break up. [*Letters* 245–48]

24   Sending a letter from her bedroom to Teddy's, Edith recapitulates recent events and tells him that "as nothing I have done seems to satisfy you for more than a few hours, I now think it is best to accede to your often repeated suggestion that we should live apart." She concludes by saying that the real estate broker and trustee, Herman Edgar, who is also her cousin, will deposit $500 a month into Teddy's Boston bank account for his personal use. She then goes to Newport for several days, where she sees Egerton Winthrop and Walter Berry. [Lewis 306–07; *Letters* 250–51]

August

"Other Times, Other Manners," *The Century Magazine*, 82: 587–94.

"Ethan Frome" [novel], *Scribner's Magazine*, 50: 151–64.

6 (Sun)   Writing to Bernard Berenson, Edith speaks of the beauty of her Lenox estate: "the stillness, the greenness, the exuberance of my flowers, the perfume of my hemlock woods, & above all the moonlight nights on my big terrace, overlooking the lake, are a very satisfying change from six months of Paris. Really, the amenities, the sylvan sweetnesses, of the Mount . . . reconcile me to America." She also tells him, however, that Teddy's "nervous excitability is very great, & the uncertainty, the ups-&-downs of the days, are inexpressibly wearing & unsettling to me." [*Letters* 252]

6   Writing to John Hugh Smith, Edith tells him that she has "decided not to sell the Mount for the present, on the chance that [Teddy] may improve & really benefit by the life here." [*Letters* 253]

26   Writing to Sara Norton, Edith tells her that "We have had a *very* large offer for the Mount . . . & have very suddenly decided to sell it. The reasons are partly economic, & partly based on Teddy's condition." Alluding to that condition, she says: "I have had a terrible two years." [*Letters* 254–55]

September

"Ethan Frome," *Scribner's Magazine*, 50: 317–34.

2 (Sat)   Edith gives Teddy legal power to rent or sell The Mount. [Lewis 313]

7   Edith leaves for Paris. When she arrives she finds a cable from Teddy telling her that he has sold The Mount. [Lewis 312; *Letters* 256]
           Edith spends a week in Paris, staying at the Crillon and seeing many people, especially Bernard Berenson. She then goes to Salsomaggiore, arriving on the 20th. [Lewis 314; *Letters* 257]

22   Writing from Salsomaggiore to Fullerton, Edith expresses her unhappiness at the sale of The Mount. [*Letters* 255–56]

30   *Ethan Frome* (New York: Scribner).
           Ethan Frome (London: Macmillan).

October

           "Ethan Frome," *Scribner's Magazine*, 50: 431–44.

4 (Wed)   Leaving Salsomaggiore with Walter Berry, Edith motors through central Italy, going through Parma, Mantua, Verona, Vicenza, Arquà, Ravenna, Rimini, and finally Florence, where she visits the Bernard Berensons at Villa I Tatti, arriving on the 15th. [Lewis 314; *Letters* 260]
           Teddy goes to a spa at French Lick, Indiana, for physical therapy. [Benstock 257]

November

7 (Tue)   Edith returns to Paris and stays at 53 Rue de Varenne. She learns that her brother, Freddy, has had a paralytic stroke, and is hospitalized. She and her brother, Harry, visit him and pay his medical expenses. [*Letters* 262; Benstock 259]

December

           "Xingu" [short story], *Scribner's Magazine*, 50: 684–96.
           Edith visits England for ten days, seeing Henry James, Gaillard Lapsley, Percy Lubbock, Howard Sturgis, and Logan Pearsall Smith. She also commissions a charcoal drawing of James from John Singer Sargent. Robert Norton accompanies her back to Paris. [Lewis 315; *Letters* 264; Benstock 260]

30 (Sat)   Writing to Sara Norton, Edith tells her that she is "immensely cheered this winter by the presence here of Daisy Chanler who is one of the people I am fondest of. My musical fervour is waxing more & more, & we go to concerts together whenever we can." She also mentions having sent her butler, Arthur White, to America to accompany Teddy to Paris, Teddy having cabled just before Christmas that he wished to come immediately. Teddy, however, postponed the trip for several weeks. [*Letters* 264–65; Lewis 316]

1912

January
Edith experiences attacks of vertigo caused by anemia. [Lewis 316]

February
"The Long Run" [short story], *Atlantic Monthly*, 109: 145–63. Teddy goes to Paris and Walter Berry returns for several weeks to the guest suite at 53 Rue de Varenne to serve as a buffer between Teddy and Edith. Teddy does not leave the apartment unless accompanied by Edith. [Lewis 316; *Letters* 268]

March
"Pomegranate Seed" [poem], *Scribner's Magazine*, 51: 284–91.
14 (Thu) Writing to Bernard Berenson, Edith tells him of feeling "the dead weight of [Teddy's state of mind], as I always do after a few weeks." [*Letters* 268–69]
16 Writing to Edith Wharton, James tells her that Sargent has completed the charcoal portrait of him that she has commissioned. He calls it "admirable." [*HJ Letters* 4: 605]
Edith drives to Spain with her Parisian friend, the Comtesse Rosa de Fitz-James, while Teddy remains in Paris with his sister, Nannie, and the butler, Arthur White. On the return journey, Edith drops off her friend at Biarritz, and revisits George Sand's Nohant before reaching Paris. [Benstock 263]

April
14 (Sun) *The Titanic* hits an iceberg and sinks on the morning of the 15th, causing the loss of 1,513 lives.

May
3 (Fri) Writing to Charles Scribner, Edith tells him that she has given her next novel, *The Reef*, to D. Appleton and Company. He is deeply saddened. [Lewis 311–12]
5 Teddy leaves 53 Rue de Varenne for the United States, never to return. [Benstock 263]
Edith returns to Salsomaggiore for the third time in twelve months. [Lewis 318]

June
Leaving Salsomaggiore with Walter Berry, Edith goes to Rome. They then go to Milan and return to Paris. [Lewis 319–20]
21 (Fri) The Mount and its land legally pass to the new owner. [Benstock 271]

July

21 (Sun)   Edith Wharton arrives at Lamb House, staying until the 23rd, after which she motors James to various places, including Windsor, Ascot, and Cliveden. When he begins to be troubled by angina, she has him driven back to Lamb House in early August, where she visits him on the 8th prior to her departure for the Continent. [*HJ Letters* 4: 621, 624]

August

11 (Sun)   Edith leaves for France and visits Jacques Emile Blanche and his wife at Offranville, near Dieppe, where she meets Jean Cocteau and then returns to Paris. [Lewis 323–24; Benstock 270]

20   Edith leaves Paris for Pougues-les-Eaux, near Bourges, to visit the Bourgets, where she stays a week, before driving through southern France, with the intention of returning to Paris around 20 September. [Benstock 271; *Letters* 277–79]

October

Edith meets the Berensons at Avignon and goes with them to Portofino, where she spends several days alone before rejoining them at Villa I Tatti, and then returning to Paris in early November. In Paris she receives a letter from Teddy, who has come with Arthur White from the United States to London, telling her not to join him there. [Lewis 327–28, 330]

November

5 (Tue)   Woodrow Wilson is elected President.

15   *The Reef* (New York: Appleton).
           The Reef (London: Macmillan).

December

Teddy, who has come to Europe with a motorcar and a chauffeur, stops briefly in Paris without notifying Edith, and then heads off to Monte Carlo and elsewhere. [Lewis 332]

24 (Tue)   Gaillard Lapsley and Percy Lubbock arrive in Paris to spend the holidays with Edith. [Benstock 274]

1913

January

"The Custom of the Country" [novel], *Scribner's Magazine*, 53: 1–24.

Edith enters into an agreement with Scribner to fund an advance payment that Scribner will offer to Henry James for his next novel. James accepts the offer, not knowing that Edith is paying for it. [Lewis 342]

17 (Fri)   Raymond Poincaré is proclaimed President of France and Edith is present at the ceremony. [Lewis 330]

February

"The Custom of the Country," *Scribner's Magazine*, 53: 186–206. Edith's cousin and legal advisor, Herman Edgar, comes to gather evidence of Teddy's infidelities in Europe and to prepare divorce papers for her. [Lewis 333; *Letters* 285]

Edith's brother, Harry, living in Paris with a woman whom he is about to marry but whom Edith has never met, breaks off relations with her, accusing her of hostility towards them. [Lewis 331; *Letters* 285]

March

"The Custom of the Country," *Scribner's Magazine*, 53: 373–95. With the help of Gaillard Lapsley, who is involved with English friends of Henry James in raising funds to celebrate his 70th birthday on 15 April, Edith composes a circular to be sent to American friends for the same purpose. It was sent to 39 people, including Henry Adams, Mrs. Jack Gardner, Senator Henry Cabot Lodge, Sara Norton, Charles Scribner, George Vanderbilt, and Barrett Wendell. [Lewis 340]

20 (Thu)   Teddy arrives in Paris and is served with a summons for a divorce decree. [Lewis 335]

28   Sending a cable to William James, Jr., Henry James, who has just learned of the plan of Edith and others to raise in America a sum of money for him as a seventieth birthday gift, expresses his "horror" and urges that William take "instant prohibitive action." [*HJ Letters* 4: 652]

28   Edith leaves Paris for a motor drive with Walter Berry through Italy and Sicily. [Lewis 339; *Letters* 289]

April

"The Custom of the Country," *Scribner's Magazine*, 53: 439–54. Edith and Berry visit the Berensons at I Tatti and then drive south to Montepulciano, Orvieto, Rome, Monte Cassino, Naples, Pompeii, throughout Sicily, and then back to Naples, after which they drive to Paris with Geoffrey Scott. [Lewis 342–45; *Letters* 291–94]

15 (Tue)   James's seventieth birthday. *The Times* reports the "Presentation to Mr. Henry James" by nearly 250 friends, in England and on the Continent, of "a letter of good wishes,

conveying the warm expression of their affectionate admiration, and asking him to sit for and accept his portrait by Mr. John S. Sargent, R. A., who is himself one of those by whom the letter is signed." The present of a golden bowl is also mentioned, "as a symbol of his friends' appreciation of his genius. The portrait, it is undersood, will eventually pass into the possession of the nation." (p. 11)

16   Edith receives a divorce decree from a Paris court on the basis of Teddy's adulterous affairs. She takes legal steps to retain the use of "Wharton" because it is her professional name. [Lewis 336; Benstock 279]

22   Writing to Fullerton from Taormina, Edith tells of having had wonderous drives through Sicily, and says: "I love the long days in the motor, & the great adventurous flights over unknown roads." [*Letters* 297–98]

29   Writing to Charles Scribner from Naples, she thanks him for his letter of 3 April informing her that Henry James has accepted the advance for *The Ivory Tower* that she funded, and enclosing James's appreciative letter acknowledging receipt of the advance. She tells Scribner that she is "delighted at the complete success of the plan, & warmly appreciative of all you have done. It did my heart good to read the letter." [*Letters* 300]

May

      "The Custom of the Country," *Scribner's Magazine*, 53: 635–53.
3 (Sat)   Writing to Morton Fullerton from Rome, where she arrived the previous evening, Edith tells him that her divorce from Teddy was obtained "on the ground of adultery in Boston, London & France." [*Letters* 300–02]
      Edith and Berry drive back to I Tatti and visit the Berensons. Berry then leaves and Edith drives to Paris with Geoffrey Scott, Berenson's protégé. [Lewis 345; Benstock 280]
20   Writing to Mary Berenson from Paris, Edith thanks her "for those golden days at Tatti," and tells her that "The journey back was beautiful to the last minute, & Mr. Scott is a traveller after my own heart." [*Letters* 302–03]
      Edith attends a performance at the Théâtre des Champs Elysées by the Ballet Russe of Igor Stravinsky's *The Rite of Spring* and calls it "extraordinary." [Lewis 346]

June

      "The Custom of the Country," *Scribner's Magazine*, 53: 756–74.

July

"The Gustom of the Country," *Scribner's Magazine*, 54: 57–74. Edith goes to England for ten days, staying at the Cavendish Hotel in London and seeing various friends, including Berenson, James, Berry, and Lapsley. She also visits Mary Hunter's Hill Hall near Epping, where she meets Victoria Sackville-West, Feodor Chaliapin, and Edward Marsh, the editor of *Georgian Poetry*. While there she is attracted by a nearby house and estate, Coopersale, and considers buying it. [Lewis 346–48]

August

"The Custom of the Country," *Scribner's Magazine*, 54: 256–67.

7 (Thu)   Edith motors to Luxembourg, where she joins Berenson for a four-week tour of Germany, visiting Cologne, Bad Nauheim, Frankfurt, Würzburg, Fulda, Weimar, and Dresden, where they see Richard Strauss's *Der Rosenkavalier*, which Edith later called "the crowning joy" of the trip. "The sensations of that evening rank with my first sight of Isadora's dancing, my first Russian ballet, my first reading of *Du Côte de chez Swann*." [Lewis 351–53; *Letters* 306, 308; *Glance* 333]

25   They arrive in Berlin, where they spend ten days and see a complete cycle of Wagner's *Der Ring des Nibelungen* as well as "a memorable performance of Tolstoy's 'Living Corpse,' and an enchanting one of the first part of Faust." She also meets the Princess of Thurn and Taxis, and Rainer Maria Rilke, "whose work I already knew and admired." [Lewis 353–54; *Glance* 332–33]

September

"The Custom of the Country," *Scribner's Magazine*, 54: 368–76.

4 (Thu)   Edith begins a motor trip back to Paris by herself. [*Letters* 312] Edith goes briefly to England, sees James, and negotiates to buy Coopersale. [Benstock 287–88]

October

"The Custom of the Country," *Scribner's Magazine*, 54: 471–83. Edith again goes to England, staying at the Ritz Hotel in London, making trips to Queen's Acre and Lamb House, and negotiating the purchase of Coopersale. [Benstock 288]

18 (Sat)   *The Custom of the Country* (New York: Scribner).

18   *The Custom of the Country* (London: Macmillan). *Letters of Charles Eliot Norton With Biographical Comment By His Daughter Sara Norton and M. A. De Wolfe Howe*, 2 vols.

(Boston and New York: Houghton Mifflin). Edith's poem, "High Pasture," appears on Vol. 2, p. 387.

November
"The Custom of the Country," *Scribner's Magazine*, 54: 622–47.

December
10 (Wed)   Edith, having contracted grippe and bronchitis, collapses while boarding the *Olympic* with Walter Berry for New York to attend the wedding of her niece, Beatrix Jones, to Max Farrand on 17 December. Berry goes on to be at the wedding, but Edith has to wait a week for another ship and misses the wedding. [Benstock 290]

Edith goes to New York on the *France* and spends time with friends in the city, especially with Minnie Jones and the Walter Maynards. [Lewis 355–56; *Letters* 313]

1914

January
7 (Wed)   Edith leaves New York on the *France* with Walter Berry. [Benstock 291; Lewis 357]

February
Edith attends a number of concerts, notably a Bach's *Well-Tempered Clavier* series and several works of Beethoven's, by which she is deeply moved. [Lewis 358]

March
A Village Romeo And Juliet. A Tale By Gottfried Keller. Translated By A. C. Bahlmann. With An Introduction By Edith Wharton (New York: Scribner). Edith's introduction appears on pp. v–xxvi.

29 (Sun)   Edith, who has come from Paris to Marseilles, sails for Algiers on the *Timgad* with Percy Lubbock as a travelling companion. They drive west through Algeria to Oran, and then east to Constantine and into Tunisia. [Lewis 359]

May
1 (Fri)   They sail from Tunis to Naples and then drive to Rome and Florence, where they visit I Tatti, after which they return to Paris. [Lewis 361; *Letters* 321, 324]

14   "The Criticism of Fiction" [article], *The Times Literary Supplement*, pp. 229–30.

June

28 (Sun)   Archduke Franz Ferdinand, heir to the Hapsburg throne, is assassinated at Sarajevo, Bosnia, by a Serbian.

July

10 (Fri)   Edith and Walter Berry leave Paris for a motor tour through Spain. [Lewis 362]

28   Austria-Hungary declares war on Serbia.

29   Edith and Walter Berry arrive back in Paris. [*Letters* 332]

August

           "The Triumph of Night" [short story], *Scribner's Magazine*, 56: 149–62.

1 (Sat)   Germany declares war on Russia.

1   A general mobilization is declared in France.

3   Germany declares war on France and invades Belgium. Britain declares war on Germany the following day. Edith organizes and raises funds for a workroom in the Rue de l'Université for unemployed seamstresses, giving them lunch and one franc a day. [Lewis 365; *Letters* 334–35]

19   Responding to Edith, who has written to Henry James of her feeling of community with the French nation, he says: "I feel on my side an immense community here, where the tension is proportionate to the degree to which we feel engaged." [*HJ Letters* 4: 715]

27   Edith sails for England, where, a month before, she had rented a country house, Stocks, near the village of Tring in Buckinghamshire, from Mrs. Humphry Ward. She leaves the Paris workroom to be managed by the young woman who had helped her establish it. [Lewis 362; *Letters* 335]

September

9 (Wed)   Edith moves to Mrs. Ward's London home on Grosvenor Place. [Price 22; Lewis 367]

24   Edith leaves Folkestone for Paris, the trip taking twenty-two hours. [Benstock 305]

27   Writing to Sara Norton, Edith tells of her return to Paris, where the manageress had left the workroom and taken the $2,000 that Edith had raised for it: "we got [the funds] back only through the intervention of the Red Cross, under whom I am working." [*Letters* 338]

30   Writing to Berenson, Edith tells him that she has been at her workroom "every day from 8 a.m. till dinner," and finds herself exhausted in the evening. [*Letters* 341]

October

Edith oversees creation of an organization eventually known as the American Hostels for Refugees that provides food and lodging for civilian refugees from the fighting, notably the Battle of the Marne (5–10 September) and that at Ypres (30 October–24 November). She gathers funds through a network of committees set up in Paris, New York, Philadelphia, and Boston, and becomes Chairman of the Franco-American General Committee. Her chief aide is Elisina Tyler. [Lewis 370–72]

December

19 (Tue)   "Edith Wharton Asks Aid for Destitute Belgians in France," *New York Herald*, p. 12.

25   *King Albert's Book. A Tribute To The Belgian King And People From Representative Men And Women Throughout The World* (Glasgow: The Daily Telegraph In Conjunction With The Daily Sketch The Glasgow Herald And Hodder And Stoughton). Edith's poem, "Belgium," appears on p. 165.

1915

January

The French Red Cross asks Edith "to report on the needs of some military hospitals near the front." [*Glance* 352]

"Introduction" to Gottfried Keller, *A Village Romeo and Juliet*, trans. A. C. Bahlmann (London: Constable).

February

18 (Thu)   The German submarine blockade of Great Britain begins.

27   Edith and Walter Berry make the first of their drives to the front, going to Châlons sur Marne, Verdun, and Bar le Duc to inspect hospitals and to deliver medical supplies. "What I saw there made me feel the urgency of telling my rich and generous compatriots something of the desperate needs of the hospitals in the war-zone, and I proposed . . . to make other trips to the front, and recount my experiences in a series of magazine articles." Eventually, she made "six expeditions, some of which actually took me into the front-line trenches." [Lewis 375–76; *Letters* 348–50; *Glance* 352–53]

March

6 (Sat)   Edith and Walter Berry make a drive to the front, bringing clothes and food to ambulances, and returning on the 10th. [*Letters* 351–53]

April

In response to a request from the Belgian Ministry of the Interior, Edith organizes and runs The Children of Flanders Rescue Committee, with the close assistance of Royall Tyler and his wife, Elisina. [Lewis 377; *Letters* 330]

May

"The Look of Paris" [article], *Scribner's Magazine*, 57: 523–31.

7 (Fri)   The British steamship *Lusitania* is torpedoed off the coast of Ireland with the loss of 1,198 lives.

"The Hymn of the Lusitania" [poem], *New York Herald*, p. 1.

14   Writing to Henry James, Edith tells him how she and Walter Berry drove to Châlons sur Marne on the 11th and then through ravaged towns to Nancy before visiting the military hospital at Pont à Mousson, "within about a mile of the German trenches, which were in full view." They intend to go "all through the Vosges to Belfort, then home." [*Letters* 354–56]

15   "Jean du Breuil de Saint-Germain" [article], *Revue Hebdomadaire*, 24: 351–61.

June

"In Argonne" [article], *Scribner's Magazine*, 57: 651–60.

19 (Sat)   Edith and Walter Berry drive north as far as Belgium, and on the 21st pass through Ypres. On the 23rd Edith has an interview with Queen Elisabeth of Belgium, "who had summoned me to talk of the Belgian child-refugees committed to our care." On the 24th she and Berry return to Paris. [Price 56–57; *Glance* 353]

25   "Edith Wharton's Work. She Wants Money to Buy Motors for the French Red Cross" [letter to the editor], *New York Times*, p. 10.

July

26 (Mon)   Henry James becomes a British citizen, but Edith has misgivings about his giving up American citizenship. [Benstock 320]

August

13 (Fri)   Edith and Walter Berry drive to the front lines in Alsace. [*Letters* 359]

25   "The Great Blue Tent" [poem], *New York Times*, p.10.

September

"Battle Sleep" [poem], *The Century Magazine*, 90: 736.

Edith goes on a three-week trip to Normandy and Brittany to work on *The Book of the Homeless*. [Benstock 319]

October

"In Lorraine and the Vosges" [article], *Scribner's Magazine*, 58: 430–42.

Edith goes to England, seeing James in London, and Sturgis and Lubbock at Queen's Acre, and returns to Paris before the 15th. It will be the last time she sees James. [Lewis 381; *Letters* 361]

November

"In the North" [article], *Scribner's Magazine*, 58: 600–10.

24 (Wed)   *Fighting France, From Dunkerque to Belfort* (New York: Scribner). It contains "The Look of Paris," "In Agonne," "In Lorraine and the Vosges," and "In the North."
Fighting France, From Dunkerque to Belfort (London: Macmillan).

25   Edith goes for a rest to the Hotel Costebelle, in Hyères, where she visits with the Bourgets, as does André Gide. Soon Robert Norton comes for a visit. [*Letters* 361–62]

28   "My Work Among the Women Workers of Paris," *New York Times Magazine*, pp. 1–2.

December

"Coming Home" [short story], *Scribner's Magazine*, 58: 702–18.

4 (Sat)   Edith, still at Hyères, receives a telegram forwarded from Paris from Henry James's amanuensis, Theodora Bosanquet, telling her that James suffered a stroke on the 2nd. Edith requests advice about coming to England or writing to James, wanting to do both but knowing that her showing intense concern would only upset him. Accordingly, she stays at Hyères. [*Letters* 363–65]

17   Writing to Gaillard Lapsley from Paris, to which she has just returned, Edith tells him that Miss Bosanquet has just written to express her doubt that James will live much longer. Edith tells Lapsley that James's "friendship has been the pride & honour of my life." [*Letters* 364–65]

1916

January

Geoffrey Scott comes from I Tatti to Edith's guest suite and stays for four months before returning to I Tatti. [Lewis 386]

22 (Sat)   *The Book of the Homeless* (New York: Scribner). Compiled and edited by Edith, it begins with a tribute by Marshal Joffre and

an introduction by Theodore Roosevelt, and contains prose, poetry, musical scores, and illustrations by almost seventy contributors, including Leon Bakst, Max Beerbohm, Jacques Emile Blanche, Paul Bourget, Rupert Brooke, Paul Claudel, Jean Cocteau, Joseph Conrad, Charles Dana Gibson, Edmund Gosse, Thomas Hardy, William Dean Howells, Henry James, Maurice Maeterlinck, Claude Monet, Paul Elmer More, Anna de Noailles, Auguste Rodin, Edmond Rostand, Theo van Rysselberghe, George Santayana, John Singer Sargent, Igor Stravinsky, William Butler Yeats, and Edith. Proceeds from the sale of the book and an auction of the manuscripts and some of the illustrations produced about $15,000 for American Hostels for Refugees and the Children of Flanders Rescue Committee. [Lewis 379–80; *Letters* 359–60]
The Book of the Homeless (London: Macmillan).

February
28 (Mon)   Henry James dies. [Lewis 383]

March
          "Kerfol" [short story], *Scribner's Magazine*, 59: 329–41.
5 (Sun)   Responding to a letter from André Gide, Edith speaks of the darkness that she is experiencing "with the extinction of the great radiance that was the soul of Henry James," and feels that "my life is so diminished by this death, this *immense absence.*" [*Letters* 371–72]
          Edith goes again to Hyères to rest and to write. Elisina and Royall Tyler manage the hostels and Lizzie Cameron assumes the secretarial duties. Edith returns to Paris at the end of April. [Price 86; *Letters* 379]
18   "Mrs. Wharton's Charity" [letter to the editor], *New York Times*, p. 10. In the letter she says that the American Hostels for Refugees is caring for 3,000 permanent refugees and has found work for 4,000 more. [*Letters* 368]
28   Edith is made a Chevalier of the Legion of Honor. [Benstock 324]

April
          Edith helps to establish an organization to cure French soldiers who have contracted tuberculosis. [Lewis 384]
6 (Thu)   Egerton Winthrop dies. [Price 89]
8   An announcement appears in *Figaro* that Edith has been made a Chevalier of the Legion of Honor by the President of France for having given assistance to French and Belgian refugees from the German invaders. [Lewis 386; *Letters* 383]

17	Writing to Minnie Jones from Beauvallon sur Mer in southern France, Edith tells of being stunned by news of the recent death of her former tutor and secretary, who had recently returned to America, Anna Bahlmann, "coming so suddenly, & so soon after Egerton's." She also mentions having received on the previous day a note from Egerton "enclosing $250 for my work! It is such a dear goodbye from the friend who never failed me." She is also saddened by the news that Robert Mintern is dying of a brain hemorrhage. [*Letters* 374; Price 91]

June

Edith urges support for Percy Lubbock's being permitted to edit the letters of Henry James. His two-volume edition appears in 1920. [*Letters* 375–77]

14 (Wed) Writing to Sara Norton, Edith tells her "I can't put much heart into anything now that the friends I loved best have been taken from me. I can't rally from the double blow of Henry James's death, & then Egerton Winthrop's, one so soon after the other." She calls them "the two wisest & best men I ever knew." [*Letters* 379]

August

Edith goes to Fontainebleau to rest and write. She returns to Paris on the 28th. [Lewis 389; *Letters* 381; Price 95]

September

Suffering from grippe, Edith goes back to Fontainebleau, returning to Paris in the middle of the month. [Price 95, 99]

19 (Tue) "A New Work for France. Mrs. Wharton on the American Treatment for Tuberculosis" [letter to the editor], *New York Times*, p. 10.

October

"Bunner Sisters" [short story], *Scribner's Magazine*, 60: 439–58.

21 (Sat) *Xingu And Other Stories* (New York: Scribner). It contains nine short stories: "Xingu," "Coming Home," "Autres Temps . . . " ["Other Times, Other Manners"], "Kerfol," "The Long Run," "The Triumph of Night," "The Choice," and "Bunner Sisters." *Xingu And Other Stories* (London: Macmillan).

November

"Bunner Sisters" [short story], *Scribner's Magazine*, 60: 575–96.

7 (Tue) Woodrow Wilson is re-elected President.

9   "For Tuberculous Soldiers. Mrs. Wharton Explains the Work of the Franco-American Sanatoria" [letter to the editor], *New York Times*, p. 12.

9   Edith's housekeeper, Catharine Gross, finds Edith lying on the floor of the apartment, having passed out from an attack of ptomaine poisoning. [Price 102]

Edith sees a good deal of Bernard Berenson, who is in Paris for a month, and also sees Jacques-Émile Blanche, Jean Cocteau, and Paul Bourget. [Lewis 389]

December

Edith has her worst attack of grippe yet. [Price 103]

18 (Mon) "Mrs. Wharton's Appeal" [letter to the editor], *New York Times*, p. 10.

1917

January

14 (Sun) "For Mrs. Wharton. Needs of the Work for Tuberculous War Victims" [letter to the editor], *New York Times*, sec. 2, p. 4.

26   "Mrs. Wharton's Work. Plans of the Committee for 'French Tuberculous War Victims'" [letter to the editor], *New York Times*, p. 8.

Germany begins unrestricted submarine warfare.

February

"Summer" [novella], *McClure's*, 48: 7–8, 10, 51–52.

3 (Sat) President Wilson severs diplomatic relations with Germany, and orders American ships to defend themselves.

13   "From Mrs. Wharton" [letter to the editor], *New York Times*, p. 10.

18   "For refugees in France" [letter to the editor], *New York Times*, sec. 7, p. 2.

Edith has another attack of grippe, which develops into pneumonia. [Price 112]

March

"Summer," *McClure's*, 48: 20–22, 62–64.

April

"Summer," *McClure's*, 48: 20–22, 65–67.

"Is There a New Frenchwoman?" [article], *Ladies' Home Journal*, 34: 12, 93.

1 (Sun)   Edith and Walter Berry make their final trip to the front, going to the valley of the Oise north of Paris, which the Germans have recently evacuated and devastated. They return to Paris on the 3rd. [Price 114]

6   "Edith Wharton Tells of German Trail of Ruin" [article], *New York Sun*, pp. 1–4.

6   The United States declares war on Germany.

11   "For Mrs. Wharton's Work in France" [quoted from a cable to Mary Cadwalader Jones], *New York Times*, p. 12.

May

           "Summer," *McClure's*, 49: 20–22, 64–67.

6 (Sun)   "Mrs. Wharton's Work. The War on Tuberculosis in France – Education of the People" [letter to the editor], *New York Times*, sec. 2, p. 3.
           Edith suffers a heart-attack. [Benstock 345]

June

           "Summer," *McClure's*, 49: 24, 26, 57–60.

July

           "Summer," *McClure's*, 49: 28, 30, 53–57.

2 (Mon)   *Summer* (New York: Appleton).
           Summer (London: Macmillan).

4   A regiment of American troops that has arrived in Paris participates in a July 4th celebration. Edith thinks it "really splendid." [Lewis 405]
           Edith visits her friend, Comtesse René de Béarn, at her chateau in Fleury, near Paris, then goes to Fontainebleau, where she stays between trips to Paris. [Price 4; Benstock 335]
           Edith receives a letter from General John J. Pershing thanking her for her war-work in France. [*Letters* 394–95]

August

           "Summer," *McClure's*, 49: 31–32, 40–42.

September

15 (Sat)   Edith leaves Paris for Madrid, where Walter Berry picks her up, and they soon go to Morocco. General Hubert Lyautey, the resident general of Morocco, has invited them to attend an exhibition of arts and crafts together with an industrial exhibition at Rabat. He also gives them a three weeks' motor tour of Morocco, where they visit Marrakech, Meknes, and Fez.

"The brief enchantment of this journey through a country still completely untouched by foreign travel, and almost destitute of roads and hotels, was like a burst of sunlight between storm-clouds." [Lewis 404–05; *Letters* 398; *Glance* 357–58]

October

Edith returns to Paris. [*Letters* 399]

November

7 (Wed)   Bolsheviks, under Nicolai Lenin, seize power in Russia.

December

"The French (As Seen by an American)" [article], *Scribner's Magazine*, 62: 676–83.

1918

January

"Les Français vus par une Américaine" [apparently Edith's translation], *Revue Hebdomadaire*, 27: 5–21.

February

Edith is invited to address the Sociétié des Conférences, made up of members of the French Academy, and delivers a lecture in French on why the United States had entered the war. [Price 143]

15 (Fri)   Writing to Bernard Berenson from Montredon, near Marseilles, Edith speaks of having enjoyed for three days "the aching beauty of this place," and tells him that she will visit Hyères and then return to Paris, which she did in mid-March. [*Letters* 403–04; Price 148]

March

2 (Sat)   "L'Amérique en Guerre" [article], *Revue Hebdomadaire*, 27: 5–28.

May

Edith suffers a second heart-attack. [Benstock 345]

June

7 (Fri)   Edith's brother, Freddy, dies in Paris. [*Letters* 405–06; Benstock 341]

July

4 (Thu)   From the terrace of the Hotel Crillon, Edith watches a grand celebratory parade down the Champs Elysées to the Tuileries. [*Letters* 406–07]
            The Belgian government awards Edith and Elisina Tyler the Médaille Reine Elisabeth for their work with refugees. [Benstock 343]

August

12 (Mon)   Death of the American, Ronald Simmons, who had been secretary of the committee for tubercular soldiers, and of whom Edith was very fond. She wrote an obituary poem for him that appeared in the November *Scribner's Magazine*, and dedicated *The Marne* and *A Son at the Front* to his memory. [Lewis 411–12; *Letters* 409]

30   "Second Greatest Fourth. So Mrs. Wharton Designates the Celebration in Paris This Year" [excerpts from a letter to Mary Cadwalader Jones], *New York Times*, p. 10.

September

            Edith's cousin, Newbold Rhinelander, serving in the Army Air Corps, dies when German planes shoot him down in France while he is returning from a bombing mission in Germany. Edith arranges a funeral for him and has him buried in the cemetery of Murville, the French village near which he died. [Lewis 414; Benstock 342]

October

            "The French We Are Learning to Know" [article], *Hearst's International Cosmopolitan*, 65: 32–33, 108–10.

26 (Sat)   "The Marne" [novel], *Saturday Evening Post*, 191: 3–5, 74, 77–78, 81–82, 85–86, 89–90.

November

            " 'On Active Service'; American Expeditionary Force (R. S., August 12, 1918)" [poem], *Scribner's Magazine*, 64: 619.

4 (Mon)   [Description of the work of American Hostels for Refugees], *Heroes of France*, no. 2, pp. 2–3.

11   The Armistice between Germany and the Allied and Associated Powers is signed in a railway coach near Compiègne, ending World War I.

December

9 (Mon)   *The Marne* (New York: Appleton).

The Marne. A Tale of the War (London: Macmillan).

28   While repair work is going on at a house, the Pavillon Colombe, that Edith has purchased in the village of St. Brice-sous-Forêt, a few miles north of Paris, she leaves Paris with Robert Norton, recently of the British Admiralty, for a stay of four months in Hyères. [Lewis 419–20; Benstock 350]

1919

January

"The Refugees" [short story], *Saturday Evening Post*, 191: 3–5, 53, 57, 61.

"The Seed of the Faith" [short story], *Scribner's Magazine*, 65: 17–33.

"The French We Are Learning to Know" [article], *Hearst's International Cosmopolitan*, 66: 40–41, 104–06.

6 (Mon)   Theodore Roosevelt dies, and Edith writes a memorial poem, "With the Tide," which appears in the *Saturday Evening Post* during March. [Benstock 350]

24 (Fri)   "You and You" [poem], *The Pittsburgh Chronicle Telegraph*, p. 6.

27   Writing to Bernard Berenson from Hyères, Edith tells him of having had to escape from Paris, and having enjoyed in Provence "days & days of healing silence, & warm sun & long walks. . . . Never have I seen it so warm, so golden, so windless & full of flowers." She rejoices in seeing no one but Norton and the Bourgets. [Letters 421]

February

"How Paris Welcomed the King" [article], *Reveille*, No. 3: 367–69.

16 (Sun)   Edith meets Rutger Jewett of Appleton, who has been working with her by correspondence, and will continue to do so for many years. [Benstock 354]

March

"The French We Are Learning to Know" [article], *Hearst's International Cosmopolitan*, 66: 40–41, 105–08.

29 (Sat)   "With the Tide" [poem], *Saturday Evening Post*, 191: 8.

April

"The French We Are Learning to Know" [article], *Hearst's International Cosmopolitan*, 66: 60–61, 94, 96–97.

Edith returns to Paris from Hyères, where she has found a house high above the town with a view of the Mediterranean,

Ste. Claire du Vieux Château, which she has leased, intending to use it as a yearly residence from December to June. [Lewis 421, 425; *Letters* 417]

June

"The French We Are Learning to Know" [article], *Hearst's International Cosmopolitan*, 67: 90–91, 132, 134–36, 138.

28 (Sat)   The Treaty of Versailles is signed, officially ending World War I.

July

"Rabat and Salé" [travel serial], *Scribner's Magazine*, 66: 1–16.

14 (Mon)   Edith sees the Bastille Day victory parade down the Champs Elysées, and finds it "so simple, so solemn, so really august." [*Letters* 423–24]

Edith has a third heart-attack. [Benstock 345]

August

"Volubilis, Moulay Idriss and Meknez" [travel serial], *Scribner's Magazine*, 66: 131–46.

7 (Thu)   Edith formally opens the Pavillon Colombe and is joined by friends including Bernard Berenson, Percy Lubbock, Gaillard Lapsley, John Hugh Smith, the Paul Bourgets, the Walter Gays, and Charles du Bos. [Lewis 426]

Edith moves into the Pavillon Colombe. [Benstock 354]

29   *French Ways and Their Meaning* (New York and London: Appleton). It contains "The French We Are Learning to Know," and "Is There a New Frenchwoman?"

September

"Writing a War Story" [short story], *Woman's Home Companion*, 46: 17–19.

"Fez" [travel serial], *Scribner's Magazine*, 66: 324–40.

October

"Marrakech" [travel serial], *Scribner's Magazine*, 66: 473–86.

"Harems and Ceremonies" [travel serial], *Yale Review*, n. s. 9: 47–71.

November

French Ways and Their Meaning (London: Macmillan).

Edith moves back to 53 Rue de Varenne for two months. [Lewis 427]

1920

January
"In Provence" [poem], *Yale Review*, n. s. 9: 346–47.
"Lyrical Epigrams" [poem], *Yale Review*, n. s. 9: 348.
Death of Howard Sturgis. [Lewis 426]
Edith goes to Hyères, where she rents a villa, Le Bocage, while work is being done on her leased home, the Château Ste. Claire, and garden. [Lewis 427]

May
Edith drives from Hyères to Paris with a good friend, Alfred de St. André. [*Letters* 431]
23 (Sun) Writing from the Rue de Varenne to Bernard Berenson, Edith says "Paris is simply awful – a kind of continuous earthquake of motor busses, trams, lorries, taxis & other howling & swooping & colliding engines, with hundreds of thousands of U. S. citizens rushing about in them & tumbling out of them at one's door." [*Letters* 431–32]

July
"Henry James in His Letters [review of Percy Lubbock's *The Letters of Henry James*]," *Quarterly Review*, 234: 188–202.
"The Age of Innocence" [novel], *Pictorial Review*, 21: 5–11, 68, 70, 74, 128.

September
"The Age of Innocence" *Pictorial Review*, 21: 20–26, 92, 95–96, 102–05, 126–35.
24 (Fri) *In Morocco* (New York: Scribner). It is dedicated to General and Madame Lyautey, and contains "Rabat and Salé," "Volubilis, Moulay Idress and Meknez," "Fez," "Marrakech," and "Harems and Ceremonies."
In Morocco (London: Macmillan).

October
"The Age of Innocence," *Pictorial Review*, 22: 23–29, 164–77.
25 (Mon) *The Age of Innocence* (New York and London: Appleton).

November
"The Age of Innocence," *Pictorial Review*, 22: 24–29, 160–64.
2 (Tue) Warren G. Harding is elected President.

December

23 (Thu)   Edith moves into the Château Ste. Claire with Gaillard Lapsley, Robert Norton, and her servants, having transferred household furnishings from 53 Rue de Varenne. [*Letters* 436–37]

26   Writing to Minnie Jones, Edith says her "little house is delicious, so friendly & comfortable, & full of sun & air; but what overwhelms us all . . . is the endless beauty of the view, or rather the views, for we look south, east & west, 'miles & miles.' " [*Letters* 436]

            Edith renews acquaintance with Philomène de Lévis-Mirepoix, a writer whom she had briefly known in Paris, and who has moved to Hyères, where they become good friends. [Lewis 438; *Letters* 434–35]

1921

January

            Walter Berry takes over Edith's lease of 53 Rue de Varenne. [Lewis 436]

February

            Death of Barrett Wendell. [Lewis 436]

17 (Thu)   Writing to Minnie Jones, Edith thanks her for arranging with Shubert to produce a stage version of *The Age of Innocence*, and praises her work as Edith's business manager in New York. [*Letters* 439–40]

April

            Bernard Berenson visits the Château Ste. Claire and finds the experience paradisial. [Lewis 437]

May

            The Age of Innocence is awarded the Pulitzer Prize of $1,000, which is given annually "for the American novel which shall best present the wholesome atmosphere of American life and the highest standard of American manners and manhood." Edith was the first woman to receive the prize. [Lewis 432–33]

June

            Edith goes to the Pavillon Colombe, where she is visited by numerous friends, including Percy Lubbock, Geoffrey Scott, Mary Hunter, and Sally and Lily Norton. [Lewis 439; *Letters* 441–42, 444]

August

6 (Sat)   Writing to Sinclair Lewis, whose novel, *Main Street*, had been rejected for the Pulitzer Prize, and who had written to congratulate Edith on her receiving the award, she warmly thanks him and expresses admiration for his novel. [*Letters* 445]

September

18 (Sun)   Edith goes to England for two weeks, seeing Robert Norton, John Hugh Smith, and Gaillard Lapsley, meeting A. E. Housman, and visiting Mary Hunter at her home of Hill Hall, near Epping Forest. [Lewis 440–41]

October

Sinclair Lewis and his wife, Grace, come from Paris to have lunch with Edith at the Pavillon Colombe. [Lewis 433]

November

Edith stays at the Hotel Crillon for several weeks. [*Letters* 448–49]

28 (Mon)   Writing to Sinclair Lewis from the Hotel Crillon, Edith gratefully accepts his proposal to dedicate *Babbitt* to her. [*Letters* 448–49]

December

5 (Mon)   Edith leaves Paris for the Château Ste. Claire. [*Letters* 449]

1922

February

"The Old Maid" [novella], *The Red Book Magazine*, 38: 31–35, 120–31.

21 (Tue)   Writing to Bernard Berenson, Edith tells him of having Percy Lubbock as a guest and planning "to get up a Hyères season for Walter [Berry], who arrives shortly." [*Letters* 450–51]

March

"The Old Maid," *The Red Book Magazine*, 38: 37–42, 118–22.

April

"The Old Maid," *The Red Book Magazine*, 38: 46–51, 166, 170.

May

"Glimpses of the Moon" [novel], *Pictorial Review*, 23: 6–11, 73, 92–102.

13 (Sat)   Writing from the Château Ste. Claire to Gaillard Lapsley, Edith tells him that "Everyone has left here but Philomène [de Lévis-Mirepoix] & her mother, who are off to Salsomaggiore for the cure next month. Minnie Jones has been with me since the middle of March, but has been away for 10 days 'doing' Provence. She gets back tonight, & we shall motor slowly northward in about 10 days." She also mentions that Sara Norton has "had a very severe operation for tumour." [Lewis 447; *Letters* 451–52]

June
"Glimpses of the Moon," *Pictorial Review*, 23: 17–23, 92–98.

July
"Glimpses of the Moon," *Pictorial Review*, 23: 17–23, 81–82.
21 (Fri)   *The Glimpses of the Moon* (New York and London: Appleton). It quickly becomes a best seller.
Sara Norton dies. [Benstock 375]

August
"Glimpses of the Moon," *Pictorial Review*, 23: 17–21, 74–78.
14 (Mon)   Edith's brother, Harry, dies. [Benstock 375]
23   Writing to Bernard Berenson, Edith tells him of the death of her brother, Harry, who "had not been allowed by his wife to see me for nearly 10 years, & the only two occasions on which I succeeded in breaking through the barriers produced only a tragic impression of some one enslaved & silenced. But he was the dearest of brothers to all my youth, & as our separation was produced by no quarrel, & no ill-will of any sort on my part, . . . my feeling is one of sadness at the years of lost affection & companionship, & all the reawakened memories of youth." [*Letters* 453]

September
2 (Sat)   Edith goes for two weeks to England to see Robert Norton, who is living as a caretaker in Henry James's Lamb House, "& then to wander about variously." [*Letters* 454]

October
22 (Sun)   Writing to Gaillard Lapsley, Edith thanks him for sending "a precious present," A. E. Housman's *Last Poems*, saying "The famous 'continuous excitement' may have vanished; but that far rarer & greater thing, 'the depth & not the tumult of the soul' has come instead." [*Letters* 458–59]

November
    Benito Mussolini assumes dictatorial powers in Italy.

December
    "A Son at the Front" [novel], *Scribner's Magazine*, 72: 643–59.
    William Gerhardi, *Futility. A Novel On Russian Themes*. Preface
    By Edith Wharton (New York: Duffield). Edith's preface
    appears on pp. 1–3.

1923

January
    "A Son at the Front," *Scribner's Magazine*, 73: 19–36.
6 (Sat) Writing to Bernard Berenson regarding James Joyce's *Ulysses*
    and T. S. Eliot's *The Waste Land*, Edith calls them merely "the
    raw material of sensation & thought." She says that the "trou-
    ble with all this new stuff is that it's à thèse: the theory comes
    first, & dominates it." She also reports that "Gaillard, Norts
    [Robert Norton] & I pursue our happy triangular existence.
    Work in the morning, a joint picnic, & generally a long walk
    over hill & dale till tea-time." [*Letters* 461]

February
    "A Son at the Front," *Scribner's Magazine*, 73: 149–66.

March
    "A Son at the Front," *Scribner's Magazine*, 73: 259–74.

April
    "A Son at the Front," *Scribner's Magazine*, 73: 389–405.
    The film version of *The Glimpses of the Moon*, starring
    Bebe Daniels, Nita Naldi, and Maurice Costello, opens to
    warm reviews in Washington, D.C. [Lewis 444; Benstock
    371–72]

May
    "A Son at the Front," *Scribner's Magazine*, 73: 547–55.
19 (Sat) Writing to Bernard Berenson from Salsomaggiore, where she
    has gone with Philomène de Lévis-Mirepoix for a cure, Edith
    tells him that Yale wishes to give her an honorary Doctor of
    Letters, and that after hesitation she has decided to attend the
    June ceremonies and accept the award, which will be the first
    honorary doctorate of letters that Yale has awarded to a
    woman. [*Letters* 466–67]

June

"A Son at the Front," *Scribner's Magazine*, 73: 688–700.

9 (Sat)   Edith embarks on the *Mauretania* from Cherbourg for New York, beginning her first trip to America since 1913. [Lewis 451; *Letters* 467]

15   Edith arrives in New York and is met by Minnie Jones, Beatrix Jones Farrand, and Max Farrand. It was to be her last trip to her homeland. [Lewis 451]

20   Edith is awarded a Doctor of Letters degree, the citation reading: "She holds a universally recognized place in the front ranks of the world's living novelists. She has elevated the level of American literature. We are proud that she is an American, and especially proud to enroll her among the daughters of Yale." [Lewis 452–53]

26   Edith boards the *Berengaria* for Cherbourg. She returns to the Pavillon Colombe on 2 July. [Lewis 453; *Letters* 468]

July

"A Son at the Front," *Scribner's Magazine*, 74: 50–62.
"New Year's Day" [novella], *The Red Book Magazine*, 41: 39–44, 156–64.

23 (Mon)   Writing to André Gide, Edith thanks him for the gift of his recent book, *Dostoïevsky*, calling it a "fascinating volume" that has "illuminated . . . this mysterious, terrible and troubling man" as no one else has done. [*Letters* 469]

August

"A Son at the Front," *Scribner's Magazine*, 74: 169–80.
"New Year's Day," *The Red Book Magazine*, 41: 54–59, 123–24, 126–31.

2 (Thu)   President Warren G. Harding dies and is succeeded by Calvin Coolidge.

September

"A Son at the Front," *Scribner's Magazine*, 74: 264–72.

7 (Fri)   *A Son at the Front* (New York: Scribner).
A Son at the Front (London: Macmillan). This was the last of Edith's books to be published by Macmillan.

30   Edith returns to the Pavillon Colombe after three weeks in England, where she spent time at Rye, Mary Hunter's Hill Hall, and London. [*Letters* 471, 473]

November

"False Dawn" [novella], *Ladies' Home Journal*, 40: 3–6, 94, 96–97, 99–100, 102, 104–05, 107.

December

"Christmas Tinsel" [autobiographical article], *Delineator*, 103: 11.

1924

January

15 (Tue) Writing to Bernard Berenson from Ste. Claire, Edith tells him that "The beloved Norts [Robert Norton] is here, painting from dawn to midnight, & Gaillard Lapsley has just left after spending his Xmas holiday here as usual." Young Henry Cabot Lodge and William Gerhardi are also visiting. [*Letters* 474–75]

February

"Temperate Zone" [short story], *Pictorial Review*, 25: 5–7, 61–62, 64, 66.

May

"The Spark" [novella], *Ladies' Home Journal*, 41: 3–5, 113–16, 119–22.

16 (Fri) *Old New York* [novellas], decorations by E. C. Caswell, 4 vols. (New York and London: Appleton). The four novellas were *False Dawn (The 'Forties), The Old Maid (The 'Fifties), The Spark (The 'Sixties),* and *New Year's Day (The 'Seventies).*

Edith goes to Salsomaggiore with Minnie Jones, and then in early June spends a week at I Tatti before going to the Pavillon Colombe. [*Letters* 476]

July

3 (Thu) Writing to Daisy Chanler, Edith tells of having visits from Minnie Jones, Gaillard Lapsley, Mary Hunter, Percy Lubbock, and Alfred de St. André. [*Letters* 476–78]

September

Edith makes a two week visit to England and spends a number of days at Hill Hall with Mary Hunter, Geoffrey Scott, Percy Lubbock, Gaillard Lapsley, and Robert Norton. It is to be her last stay at Hill Hall because Mary's husband, Charles, was to die some months later, and she was to sell it. [Lewis 463]

October

"The Mother's Recompense" [novel], *Pictorial Review*, 26: 5–9, 28–30, 128.

November

"The Mother's Recompense," *Pictorial Review*, 26: 23–27, 54–56, 59–60, 62.

4 (Tue)   Calvin Coolidge is re-elected President.

December

"The Mother's Recompense," *Pictorial Review*, 26: 21–25, 60, 62, 64, 67–68, 70.

"In General" [article], *Scribner's Magazine*, 76: 571–77.

1925

January

"The Mother's Recompense," *Pictorial Review*, 26: 21–25, 31–32, 34.

"Marcel Proust" [article], *Yale Review*, n. s. 14: 209–22.

Edith is awarded the Gold Medal of the American Academy of Arts and Letters, which was given annually for "distinguished service to art or letters in the creation of original work." [Lewis 460; Benstock 385]

February

"The Mother's Recompense," *Pictorial Review*, 26: 21–25, 118–19, 120–30.

March

"Bewitched" [short story], *Pictorial Review*, 26: 14–16, 60–64, 69. Sinclair Lewis visits Edith at Ste. Claire. [Lewis 466]

April

"Miss Mary Pask" [short story], *Pictorial Review*, 26: 8–9, 75–76.

"Telling a Short Story" [article], *Scribner's Magazine*, 77: 344–49.

24 (Fri)   *The Mother's Recompense* (New York and London: Appleton).

May

"Constructing a Novel" [article], *Scribner's Magazine*, 77: 456–61. Edith drives through the Pyrenees on the way to the Pavillon Colombe with Robert Norton. [*Letters* 483]

June

"Constructing A Novel" [article], *Scribner's Magazine*, 77: 611–19.

8 (Mon)   Writing from the Pavillon Colombe to F. Scott Fitzgerald,
            Edith thanks him for sending her a copy of *The Great Gatsby*,
            which had recently been published by Scribner. She admired
            his novel, but when he called on her a few days later, he was
            a bit inebriated and she found his behavior "awful." [*Letters*
            481–82].

August

"Velvet Ear-Muffs" [short story], *The Red Book Magazine*, 45:
39–45, 140–48.

September

Edith drives with Walter Berry to Compostella. [*Letters* 488]

October

"Character and Situation in the Novel" [article], *Scribner's
Magazine*, 78: 394–99.

9 (Fri)   *The Writing of Fiction* (New York and London: Scribner). It was
            dedicated to Gaillard Lapsley and contains "In General,"
            "Telling a Short Story," "Constructing a Novel," "Character
            and Situation in the Novel," and "Marcel Proust."

1926

February

"The Young Gentlemen" [short story], *Pictorial Review*, 27:
29–30, 84–91.

March

27 (Sat)   *Here and Beyond*, decorations by E. C. Caswell (New York and
            London: Appleton). It contains six short stories: "Miss Mary
            Pask," "The Young Gentlemen," "Bewitched," "The Seed of
            the Faith," "The Temperate Zone," and "Velvet Ear-Pads."

27   "A Bottle of Evian" [short story], *Saturday Evening Post*, 198:
            8–10, 116, 121–22.

31   The *Osprey*, an English steam yacht that Edith has chartered,
            leaves from Hyères for a nine week cruise through the
            Mediterranean and Aegean. Edith's guests are Logan Pearsall
            Smith, Daisy Chanler, Robert Norton, and Harry Lawrence,
            director of the Medici Society in London. Edith later recalled
            that the day was "serene and sunny, and we were a congenial
            party, with lots of books, a full set of Admiralty charts, a
            stock of good provisions and *vins du pays* in the hold, and
            happiness in our hearts. From that day until we disembarked

two months and one week later, I lived in a state of euphoria." [Benstock 390; *Glance* 372]

April

11 (Sun)   Writing to Gaillard Lapsley from the *Osprey* in the Gulf of Corinth, Edith tells him that at night they read aloud *The Odyssey* or *Gentlemen Prefer Blondes*. She, Lapsley, and Robert Norton had pronounced Anita Loos's novel, published in 1925, as "the greatest novel since *Manon Lescaut*." [*Letters* 489–91]

June

Edith and her friends return to Ste. Claire. [*Glance* 372]

August

Minnie Jones and Geoffrey Scott visit Edith at the Pavillon Colombe. [*Letters* 491–92]

September

Edith and Walter Berry drive through northern Italy. [Lewis 470]

October

23 (Sat)   *Twelve Poems* (London: Medici Society). It contains "Nightingales in Florence," "Mistral in the Maquis," "Les Salettes [December 1923]," "Dieu d'Amour [A Castle in Cyprus]," "Segesta," "The Tryst [1914]," "Battle Sleep," "Elegy [1918]," "With the Tide [6th January 1919]," "La Folle du Logis," "The First Year [All Souls' Day]," and "Alternative Epitaphs."

November

17 (Sun)   Edith returns to Ste. Claire. [*Letters* 495]

December

Walter Berry, Robert Norton, and Gaillard Lapsley visit Edith at Ste. Claire for Christmas. [Lewis 471]

Robert Bliss, an American diplomat, and his wife, Mildred, who had been an associate of Edith's during the War, initiate efforts to secure the Nobel Prize for her. They contact a number of distinguished people, including Arthur Hadley, president emeritus of Yale, Chief Justice Howard Taft, Elihu Root, Lord Balfour, Paul Bourget, and the French diplomat, Jules Cambon. [Lewis 372, 481–82]

With the legal help of Walter Berry, Edith purchases Ste. Claire. [Benstock 394; *Letters* 498]

1927

January

William Lyon Phelps draws up a statement addressed to the Nobel Prize Committee that is then signed by six other Yale English professors nominating Edith "as the foremost living creative literary artist of America," but the Committee does not respond favorably. It gives two awards, one to Grazua Deledda, and the other to Henri Bergson. [Lewis 481–82]

February

"Twilight Sleep" [novel], *Pictorial Review*, 28: 8–11, 78–94.

March

"Twilight Sleep," *Pictorial Review*, 28: 19–21, 96–110.
Geoffrey Scott comes to visit Edith at Ste. Claire and stays for two months. [Lewis 474]

April

"Twilight Sleep," *Pictorial Review*, 28: 14–15, 85–102.

May

"Twilight Sleep," *Pictorial Review*, 28: 24–25, 91–92, 94, 97, 104, 120–28.

13 (Fri)   *Twilight Sleep* (New York and London: Appleton).
20–21   Charles A. Lindberg flies solo across the Atlantic, landing in Paris.

June

Edith goes to the Pavillon Colombe. [Lewis 476]

July

"The Great American Novel" [article], *Yale Review*, n. s. 16: 646–56.

September

Edith visits Salsomaggiore for two weeks and then motors back to Paris. [*Letters* 501; Benstock 400]

October

2 (Sun)   Walter Berry suffers a stroke and Edith comes from the Pavillon Colombe to the Hotel Crillon in Paris to be near him. [Lewis 476]
12   Walter Berry dies. [Lewis 477]

12   Writing to her English friend, John Hugh Smith, Edith tells
            him of Walter Berry's death and says: "Yesterday afternoon
            I held him in my arms, & talked to him of old times, & he
            pressed my hand & remembered." [*Letters* 503]

15   Writing again to John Hugh Smith, Edith tells him "I am
            proud of having kept such a perfect friendship . . . & always
            to have felt that, through all the coming & going of things in
            his eager ambitious life, I was there, in . . . the place of perfect
            understanding." She also tells him that Robert "Norton is
            staying with me, & won't leave till after the funeral. He has
            been kindness itself." [*Letters* 504–05]

29   Walter Berry's ashes are buried in the Cimitière des Gonards
            at Versailles, with Edith present. She felt "The stone closed
            over all my life." [Lewis 478]

November

"Atrophy" [short story], *Ladies' Home Journal*, 44: 8–9,220–22.
Edith goes to Ste. Claire. [Benstock 405]

December

Royall Tyler, Gaillard Lapsley, Robert Norton, the Bernard
Berensons, and Nicky Mariano, visit Edith at Ste. Claire for
Christmas. [Lewis 480]

1928

January

"Garden Valedictory" [poem], *Scribner's Magazine*, 83: 81.

February

7 (Tue)   Teddy Wharton dies. He leaves his estate of $56,685 to the
            nurse who had been taking care of him. Edith felt that it is "a
            happy release, for the real Teddy went years ago, & these
            survivals of the body are ghastly beyond expression." She also
            said "I am thankful to think of him at peace after all the
            weary agitated years." [Lewis 480–81; *Letters* 514–15]

April

"Mr. Jones" [short story], *Ladies' Home Journal*, 45: 3–5, 108,
111–12, 114, 116.
"The Children" [novel], *Pictorial Review*, 29: 11–16, 60–78.

May

5 (Sat)   "After Holbein" [short story], *Saturday Evening Post*, 200: 6–7,
            179, 181–82, 185–86, 189.

"The Children," *Pictorial Review*, 29: 24–29, 56, 61–70.
Edith, with Daisy Chanler, journeys to Spain and visits the Prado. [*Letters* 519; Benstock 413]

June

"The Children," *Pictorial Review*, 29: 25–30, 45–57.

July

"The Children," *Pictorial Review*, 29: 22–25, 68, 82–87.
Edith goes to England for two weeks, visiting Robert Norton at Lamb House, and going briefly to London and to Tintagel. [Lewis 482–83; *Letters* 516–17]

August

"Had I Been Only" [poem], *Scribner's Magazine*, 84: 215.
"The Children," *Pictorial Review*, 29: 22–25, 64–72.
Logan Pearsall Smith brings Desmond MacCarthy to meet Edith at Pavillon Colombe. [Lewis 485]

September

1 (Sat) "Hudson River Bracketed" [novel], *Delineator*, 113: 12–14, 88–96.

1 *The Children* (New York and London: Appleton). It is dedicated to her "Patient Listeners at Ste. Claire."
The Children becomes a Book-of-the-Month Club selection and Edith earns $95,000 in two months from book sales and film rights – more money than she had received from any previous novel. [Lewis 484; *Letters* 509]

October

"Dieu d'Amour" [short story], *Ladies' Home Journal*, 45: 6–7, 216, 219–20, 223–24.
"Hudson River Bracketed," *Delineator*, 113: 16–17, 76–85.

November

"William C. Brownell" [article], *Scribner's Magazine*, 84: 596–602.
"Hudson River Bracketed," *Delineator*, 113: 18–19, 101–08.

3 (Sat) "A Cycle of Reviewing" [article], *Spectator*, 141, supplement, pp. 44–45.

6 Herbert Hoover is elected President.

27 The stage version of *The Age of Innocence* by Margaret Barnes, and starring Katharine Cornell, successfully opens in New York and runs until mid-June 1929, after which it goes on the road and plays in nine cities. [Lewis 487; Benstock 410]

December
  "Hudson River Bracketed," *Delineator*, 113: 16–17, 64–74.

1929

January
  "Hudson River Bracketed," *Delineator*, 114: 15–16, 68–73.

February
  "Hudson River Bracketed," *Delineator*, 114: 20–21, 101–05.
  Edith's gardens at Ste. Claire are largely destroyed by severe cold and gales, but are restored by Christmas. [Lewis 487, 489]
15 (Fri) Edith accepts an offer from the President of Columbia University, Nicholas Murray Butler, to present her with an honorary Doctor of Letters in June, and she books passage to New York. [Lewis 488; *Letters* 519]

March
  "Hudson River Bracketed," *Delineator*, 114: 25–26, 83–89.
  "Visibility in Fiction" [article], *Yale Review*, n. s. 18: 480–88.
4 (Mon) In southern France Edith contracts a severe chill that develops into nausea, fever, heart palpitations, and thorough exhaustion. The breakdown continues for several months, preventing writing and forcing cancellation of the New York trip. During her illness she is cared for by Robert Norton and Elisina Tyler, and in early May by Daisy Chanler. [Lewis 488–89]

April
  "Hudson River Bracketed," *Delineator*, 114: 25, 70–79.

May
  "Hudson River Bracketed," *Delineator*, 114: 37–38, 108–13.
  Late in the month, Edith travels north to Paris and the Pavillon Colombe. [Lewis 489]

June
  "Hudson River Bracketed," *Delineator*, 114: 37–38, 58–65.

July
  "Hudson River Bracketed," *Delineator*, 115: 34, 83–87.
  Edith goes to England, visiting London and Lamb House. [Lewis 489]

August
> "Hudson River Bracketed," *Delineator*, 115: 35–36, 54.
> Death of Geoffrey Scott. [Lewis 489]

September
> "Hudson River Bracketed," *Delineator*, 115: 49, 105–08.

October
> "Hudson River Bracketed," *Delineator*, 115: 41, 117–19.
> Edith goes to Ste. Claire. [Lewis 489]

25 (Fri) Writing to Elisina Tyler, Edith tells of her pleasure in having a gramophone, and in having played music for Elisina's son, William, visiting from Harrow: "He caught me in a guilty honeymoon with a gramophone, & we listened to Mozart, Weber & the Rosenkavalier." [*Letters* 524]

29 The New York stock market collapses and initiates the Great Depression.

November
> "Hudson River Bracketed," *Delineator*, 115: 49, 102–04.

8 (Fri) *Hudson River Bracketed* (New York and London: Appleton). It was dedicated to John Hugh Smith.
> Edith goes to Ste. Claire. [*Letters* 525]

December
> "Hudson River Bracketed," *Delineator*, 115: 44, 90–93.
> Edith's Christmas guests at Ste. Claire are Robert Norton, Gaillard Lapsley, John Hugh Smith, Bernard Berenson, and Nicky Mariano. [Lewis 493]

1930

January
> "Hudson River Bracketed," *Delineator*, 116: 38, 83–85.

February
> "Hudson River Bracketed," *Delineator*, 116: 44, 84–96.
> Daisy Chanler arrives at Ste. Claire. [Benstock 418]

March
> Edith and Daisy Chanler visit Spain. [Lewis 494; *Letters* 526]

August

8 (Fri)   Writing to Gaillard Lapsley from the Pavillon Colombe, Edith tells of having had "10 peaceful & harmonious days" with John Hugh Smith, and of their having seen the Indre, Poitou, and Anjou, and having come back "with our eyes full of the glories of Mantes." She also tells of having Minnie Jones and Mary Berenson as her current guests. [*Letters* 528]

September

Edith goes to Salsomaggiore and I Tatti, where she meets Kenneth and Jane Clark. [Lewis 494, 497; *Letters* 528–30, 539]

October

21 (Tue)   *Certain People* (New York and London: Appleton). It was dedicated to Edward Sheldon, and contains six short stories: "Atrophy," "A Bottle of Perrier," "After Holbein," "Dieu d'Amour," "The Refugees," and "Mr. Jones."

November

"Diagnosis" [short story], *Ladies' Home Journal*, 47: 8–9, 156, 159–60, 162.

Morton Fullerton writes to Edith expressing his liking for the *Hudson River Bracketed*, and their affection reemerges. [*Letters* 530–31]

December

12 (Fri)   Sinclair Lewis accepts the Nobel Prize in Stockholm.

Aldous and Maria Huxley and Cyril and Jean Connolly visit Edith at Ste. Claire. [Lewis 497]

1931

January

11 (Sun)   Writing to Morton Fullerton, Edith asks him to forward a letter of hers addressed to the Editor of *The Paris Herald*, appealing for charitable donations to assist people in the settlement of Lutèce, near Garges-lès-Gonesse, who are suffering from notable privation. Fullerton did so and the letter was published. [*Letters* 531–32]

February

8 (Sun)   Edith invites Morton Fullerton to Ste. Claire, but though he is unable to come, he later pays visits to the Pavillon Colombe. [Lewis 500]

March

Kenneth and Jane Clark visit Edith at Ste. Claire. [Lewis 498]

April

3 (Fri)   Writing to Gaillard Lapsley from Ste. Claire, Edith tells of having had "the really delightful Kenneth Clarks for a short visit." She also mentions her plan to go to Rome, perhaps in May, "to stay with the Garretts," John Garrett being the American Ambassador to Italy. She delayed the trip, however. [*Letters* 537–38]

25   "Pomegranate Seed" [short story], *Saturday Evening Post*, 203: 6–7, 109, 112, 116, 119, 121, 123.

June

Edith goes to the Pavillon Colombe. [*Letters* 539]

July

Edith goes to England for three weeks, seeing the Clarks, Desmond MacCarthy, Arthur Waley, Sacheverell Sitwell, Dame Edith Sitwell, Osbert Sitwell, Harold Nicholson, Lord David Cecil, Sir James Barrie, H. G. Wells, and her old friend, Mary, now Countess of Wemyss. [Lewis 499; *Letters* 539]

November

18 (Wed)   Writing to Daisy Chanler from Rome, Edith, who has not visited Rome since 1914, tells her that "every moment has been filled with beauty & delight." Having gone to I Tatti about three weeks before, she has come to Rome with Nicky Mariano for a week, and will return to I Tatti before going to Hyères. [*Letters* 541]

1932

January

17 (Sun)   Writing to Bernard Berenson from Ste. Claire, Edith tells him of motoring to Marseilles on the 15th to hear a concert by Wanda Landowska, whom she brought to Ste. Claire on the following day, and whose greetings she sends to Berenson and Mary. [*Letters* 543]

23   Writing to Berenson, Edith tells of just being back from a three-day trip, after Landowska's departure, to Nice with Robert Norton to attend a Mozart festival, where they heard "Die Entführung & Figaro, the latter simply *ravishing*." She also says, "I am very sorry that Lytton Strachey is dead. He

was, with Aldous Huxley, the only light left in that particular quarter of the heavens." [*Letters* 544–45]

February

"Her Son" [short story], *Scribner's Magazine*, 91: 65–72, 113–28.
"The Gods Arrive" [novel], *Delineator*, 120: 8–9, 40–42, 45–46, 48, 50.

March

"The Gods Arrive," *Delineator*, 120: 10–11, 66–68, 70, 72, 74, 76, 78.

25 (Fri)   Writing to Daisy Chanler from Ste. Claire, Edith speaks of "dear [Louis] Gillet," the art curator and historian, and literary critic, "who was here last month, & is returning after Easter." She is also expecting Bernard Berenson, Nicky Mariano, Reginald and Molly Nicholson, and Kenneth and Jane Clark, "& when my visitors scatter I shall probably dip down into Italy for a month." [*Letters* 546–47]

April

"The Gods Arrive," *Delineator*, 120: 16–17, 78–83, 94.

May

"The Gods Arrive," *Delineator*, 120: 18–19, 89–91, 93–97.

23 (Mon)   Writing to John Hugh Smith from Rome, Edith tells him of having "left Hyères on the 8th, & motored to I Tatti, to spend two days, & see Mary B," who has not been well. "I came on here, & B.B. & Nicky joined me about a week ago. Every minute has been rich in enjoyment." [*Letters* 548–49]

30   Edith arrives in Assisi, having gone through Spoleto and Spello. [*Letters* 550–51]

June

"The Gods Arrive," *Delineator*, 120: 12–13, 74–81.

4 (Sat)   Writing to Mary Berenson from Salsomaggiore, Edith tells of having gone from Assisi to Loreto, Recanati, Rimini, Ravenna, and Ferrara. "I hadn't seen any of them in years, & flying from one to the other over painless perfect roads makes it all so different fr. the old creaking travel days." After spending two nights at Salsomaggiore, she plans to take "the train to Paris tomorrow." [*Letters* 553–54]

July

"The Gods Arrive," *Delineator*, 120: 12–14, 53–55, 64–67.

19 (Tue)   Writing to Jane Clark from London, Edith sends thanks for her visit to the Clarks' home near Oxford, and for Kenneth's showing her through the Ashmolean Museum, of which he is Keeper. [*Letters* 554–55]

August
"The Gods Arrive," *Delineator*, 120: 18–19, 52–53, 60–64.

September
"The Writing of *Ethan Frome*" [article], *Colophon*, part II, no. 4, n. p.

16 (Fri)   *The Gods Arrive* (New York and London: Appleton).

October
The Kenneth Clarks have twins. Edith becomes godmother to Colin and Nicky Mariano to Colette. [Lewis 498]

November
3 (Tue)   Franklin D. Roosevelt is elected President.

12   "A Glimpse" [short story], *Saturday Evening Post*, 205: 16–17, 64–65, 67, 70, 72.

25   Writing to Kenneth Clark from Ste. Claire, where she has arrived the previous day, Edith mentions the baptismal present that she has sent to Colin: a silver mug that was her mother's. [*Letters* 556–57]

December
"Joy in the House" [short story], *Nash's Pall Mall Magazine*, 90: 6–9, 72–75.

1933

January
"In a Day" [short story], *Woman's Home Companion*, 60: 7–8, 46. Mary Hunter dies. [Lewis 509]

30 (Mon)   Adolf Hitler is made Chancellor of Germany.

February
"In a Day," *Woman's Home Companion*, 60: 15–16, 104, 106, 118.

March
17 (Fri)   *Human Nature* (New York and London: Appleton). It is dedicated to Bernard Berenson and contains "Her Son," "The Day

of the Funeral" ["In a Day"], "A Glimpse," "Joy in the House," and "Diagnosis."

April

"Confessions of a Novelist" [autobiographical article], *Atlantic Monthly*, 151: 385–92.

May

29 (Mon)   Edith's maid, Elise Duvlenck, dies. (*Letters* 561)

June

Edith goes north to Paris and then to England for several weeks. [Lewis 514]

July

10 (Sat)   Writing to Bernard Berenson from Stanway, Edith tells him that she "came to England nearly 3 weeks ago, & the complete change of scene & society has done me lots of good." During her stay in England she has gone for "a five days' trip to Wales with G. Lapsley, & that also delighted me. We had never either of us been to Wales before." She also tells him that she is visiting Stanway with Robert Norton, "whom I first met here 25 years ago! We found ourselves in the Visitors' Book at that distant date, & kissed again with tears!" After a brief stay in London, she plans to leave for the Pavillon Colombe at St. Brice on the 13th. [*Letters* 562–63]

August

28 (Mon)   Writing to Gaillard Lapsley from Salzburg, where she has gone for six days to attend the summer music festival, she speaks of having enjoyed the musical performances of Bruno Walter and Lotte Lehmann. She also unexpectedly meets Percy Lubbock, but his wife, Sybil, avoids seeing Edith. [*Letters* 566–67]

28   Edith also writes to Kenneth Clark, congratulating him on being appointed Director of the National Gallery in London. [*Letters* 567–68]

29   Edith returns home to the Pavillon Colombe. [*Letters* 568]

October

"A Backward Glance" [autobiographical article], *Ladies' Home Journal*, 50: 5–6, 131–32, 134–37.

Catharine Gross, Edith's housekeeper-companion since 1884, having been stricken with dementia, dies and is buried at Hyères next to Elise Duvlenck. [Lewis 54, 513–14]

20 (Fri) Writing to Daisy Chanler fom The Hague, Edith tells her "My dear old Gross died peacefully at Hyères about a fortnight ago, & though I wd not have had her live longer her loss makes my life seem emptier than ever, & I had to go away for a while." "Still," she says, "I've had a thrilling week, & seen oh such things." She mentions having spent a weekend near Brussels and since then having "devoted myself strictly to Amsterdam (which enchanted me), Haarlem & the Hague. If it's not too cold I'm going to Delft tomorrow, & home to St. Brice the day after." [*Letters* 570–71]

November

"A Backward Glance," *Ladies' Home Journal*, 50: 16–17, 90, 92–93, 95.

December

"A Backward Glance," *Ladies' Home Journal*, 50: 15–16, 69.
"The Looking-Glass" [short story], *Hearst's International-Cosmopolitan*, 95: 32–35, 157–59.
John Hugh Smith, Gaillard Lapsley, Robert Norton, and Steven Runciman visit Edith for the holidays. [Lewis 513]

1934

January

"A Backward Glance," *Ladies' Home Journal*, 51: 19, 73, 78, 80.
27 (Sat) "Tendencies in Modern Fiction" [article], *Saturday Review of Literature*, 10: 433–34.

February

"Bread Upon the Waters" [short story], *Hearst's International-Cosmopolitan*, 96: 28–31, 90, 92, 94, 96, 98.
12 (Mon) There is a general strike in France after six days of bloody rioting in Paris.
12 Writing to Bernard Berenson from Ste. Claire, Edith reports having been listening feverishly to the wireless during the first days of the rioting. [*Letters* 574–75]

February–March

"A Backward Glance," *Ladies' Home Journal*, 51: 23, 90, 95, 97.

April

"A Backward Glance," *Ladies' Home Journal*, 51: 49–50, 52, 54, 56.

7 (Sat)	"Permanent Values in Fiction" [article], *Saturday Review of Literature*, 10: 603–04.
10	Writing to Minnie Jones from Ste. Claire, Edith tells her of having declined Columbia University's renewed invitation to accept an honorary degree. "I had made up my mind to go, more to please you than myself, for I am too old to care for Academic honours; but the truth is, the political situation here is too unsettled for me to wish to leave next month." She also tells of planning to "leave about April 25 for I Tatti, & then, if things are quiet in France, for Rome. If things seem more unsettled I will come back here." [*Letters* 576–77]
27	*A Backward Glance* (New York and London: Appleton-Century). It is dedicated "To the Friends Who Every Year on All Souls' Night Come and Sit with Me by the Fire."

May

Having visited I Tatti, Edith goes with Bernard Berenson and Nicky Mariano to Rapallo, Florence, and Rome, where she contracts chills and fever that keep her in her hotel room for her entire two-week stay in Rome. [Lewis 519]

July

11 (Wed)	Writing to John L. B. Williams, who was replacing the ailing Rutger Jewett on the Appleton editorial staff, Edith expresses her wish to cancel the book contract for the publication of her novel in progress, *The Buccaneers*, so that she can find another publisher, and she complains that Appleton fails to advertize adequately. A lengthy reply on 25 July by D. W. Hiltman, Chairman of the Board at Appleton, summarizes her earnings for the works published by Appleton for the previous 20 years ($578,905.04), and asks her to withdraw her request. Edith remained with Appleton. [*Letters* 580–82; Benstock 440]
25	Englebert Dollfuss, the Austrian Chancellor, is assassinated.

August

2 (Thu)	Paul von Hindenburg, President of the German Republic, dies, and Hitler becomes absolute dictator.

September

Edith visits Lady Wemyss (the former Lady Mary Elcho) in Scotland and makes a tour of Scotland. In London she is shown about the National Gallery by Kenneth Clark. [Lewis 517–18; *Letters* 577]

October

The Age of Innocence, a talking film starring Irene Dunne, opens at Radio City Music Hall in New York, but has only a short run. [Benstock 438]

27 (Sat) "A Reconsideration of Proust" [article], *Saturday Review of Literature*, 11: 233–34.

November

10 (Sat) "Roman Fever" [short story], *Liberty*, 11: 10–14.

17 Writing to Minnie Jones from the Hotel Crillon, Edith says she will leave that evening on a "flight to Italy." [*Letters* 583]

December

During the month and in the early new year, Edith is visited at Ste. Claire by Louis Bromfield, Beatrix Farrand, John Hugh Smith, Robert Norton, Gaillard Lapsley, Bernard Berenson, the Aldous Huxleys, the Charles de Noailles, the Kenneth Clarks, and Lady Wemyss. [Lewis 516–17, 519]

1935

January

7 (Mon) *The Old Maid*, dramatized by Zoë Akins, and with Judith Anderson and Helen Menken in the leading roles, opens in New York at the Empire Theatre and is very successful. It won a Pulitzer Prize in May, continued through the summer, and then went on the road. In 1936 it was being produced in England. [Lewis 528–29]

April

"Poor Old Vincent!" [short story], *The Red Book Magazine*, 64: 20–23, 116–19.

11 (Thu) Edith apparently has a stroke and for a time loses sight in her left eye. [Lewis 519]

May

Elisina Tyler comes to Ste. Claire and stays with Edith until early June, by which time Edith has largely recovered her eyesight, and been able to walk and to go for drives. [*Letters* 585–87]

June

Elisina and Edith drive north to Paris and the Pavillon Colombe at St. Brice. [Lewis 519]

July

25 (Thu)   Writing to John Hugh Smith, Edith tells him that she and Elisina have visited a private showing of Italian paintings at the Petit Palais, saying, "The shock of that great tidal wave of beauty, after nearly 4 months of isolation, was almost more than I could bear." She also says that "Elisina leaves today, & my poor old sister-in-law [Minnie Jones] arrives this afternoon for a fortnight." [*Letters* 587–88]

September

22 (Sun)   Mary Cadwalader Jones ["Minnie"], who had gone to England after visiting Edith at the Pavillon Colombe, dies in a London hotel. [Lewis 519; Benstock 445]

30   Writing to Bernard Berenson from the Pavillon Colombe, Edith tells him that she has just returned from Minnie's burial: "I have had an exhausting week in London, but now she is quietly at rest in the lovely little churchyard of Aldbury, where we buried her among her old friends, the Wards and Arnolds." [*Letters* 590]

1936

January

6 (Mon)   *Ethan Frome*, dramatized by Owen and Donald Davis, and staged by Guthrie McClintic, with Raymond Massey, Pauline Lord, and Ruth Gordon, opens very successfully in Philadelphia. It then runs for four months in New York, and afterwards goes on the road. [Lewis 529; Benstock 446]

20 (Mon) King George V of England dies and is succeeded by Edward VIII.

February

19 (Wed) Writing to Gaillard Lapsley from Ste. Claire, Edith tells him of the success of her two plays, *The Old Maid* and *Ethan Frome*, the former in New York and the latter going west and "coming out in England, in the provinces, next month, & in London (produced by [Charles Blake] Cochran) in April." She also speaks of having had "a nice long visit from Robert [Norton]," and two brief visits from John Hugh Smith. Now she expects visits from Bernard Berenson and Nicky Mariano, then Reginald and Molly Nicholson. "Then come (later) the Blisses, the Clarks & Lady Wemyss [and] the Boccon-Gibods." André Boccon-Gibod had been her Paris divorce lawyer and had served on the hostels committee during the war. She

expects to "stay here till the middle of May. I had thought of an after-Easter dash to Spain – but I see Spain has gone red! – What a world." [*Letters* 574, 590–92]

March

"Unconfessed Crime" [short story], *Story-Teller*, 58: 64–85.

7 (Sat)   Hitler sends troops into the Rhineland in defiance of the Versailles treaty.

April

24 (Fri)   *The World Over* (New York and London: Appleton-Century). "For my dear sister MARY CADWALADER JONES who for so many years faithfully revised me in proof and indulgently read me in print." It contains seven short stories: "Charm Incorporated," "Pomegranate Seed," "Permanent Wave," "Confession," "Roman Fever," "The Looking-Glass," and "Duration."

May

23 (Sat)   Writing to Elisina Tyler, Edith gives her detailed *"Instructions after my death."* These include a wish for a funeral service at the American Episcopal Cathedral of the Holy Trinity in Paris, with three hymns sung: "Lead, Kindly Light," "Art Thou Weary," and "O Paradise." She also asks for the following pall-bearers: Royall Tyler, Kenneth Clark, John Hugh Smith, Gaillard Lapsley, Robert Norton, André Boccon-Gibod, Louis Metman, and Louis Gillet. Finally, she indicates her wish to be buried at the Cimetière des Gonards at Versailles, "as near as possible to Walter Berry's grave. I wish a grave stone like his, with my birth & death dates . . . & Ave Crux Spes Unica engraved under it." [*Letters* 594–96]

June

21 (Wed)   "Souvenirs du Bourget d'Outre-mer" [article], *Revue Hebdomadaire*, 45: 266–86.

July

Edith is in England, where she attends the festival at Glyndebourne, sees the Kenneth Clarks, the Reginald Nicholsons, E. M. Forster, Max Beerbohm, H. G. Wells, Lord David Cecil, Herbert and Cynthia Asquith, and Lady Sybil Cutting, and she stays at Stanway with Lady Wemyss. [Lewis 529; *Letters* 596–97]

20 (Mon)   Outbreak of the Spanish Civil War.

November
2 (Tue)   Franklin D. Roosevelt is re-elected President.

December
           Edith reaches Ste. Claire after spending two weeks at I Tatti.
           [Lewis 529]
10 (Thu)   Edward VIII abdicates and is succeeded by George VI.
           Edith is joined at Ste. Claire for the holidays by Gaillard
           Lapsley, Robert Norton, and John Hugh Smith. [Benstock 450]

1937

April
9 (Fri)   Writing to Bernard Berenson from Ste. Claire, Edith tells him
           of having suffered "*three* successive attacks of flu – in January,
           March, & now, a queer sort of relapse, which has left me as
           weak as a cat." [*Letters* 603]

May
           Lady Mary Wemyss dies in an English nursing home.
           [Lewis 530]
           Edith drives north and stops at the chateau of Ogden
           Codman, south of Paris, where, on about 1 June, she has a
           stroke. [Lewis 530]

June
3 (Thu)   Edith is taken from Codman's chateau to the Pavillon
           Colombe. Elisina Tyler comes the next day to be with her.
           [Lewis 530]

July
           Edith makes a slight recovery. She has been visited by the
           Kenneth Clarks, John Hugh Smith, Royall Tyler, Robert
           Norton, and William Royall Tyler and his wife. [Lewis 530]

August
11 (Wed)   Death of Edith Wharton. She is buried in the Cimetière des
           Gonards in Versailles, near the grave of Walter Berry. [Lewis
           531–32]

October
15 (Fri)   *Ghosts* (New York and London: Appleton-Century). It contains
           "Preface" and eleven short stories: "All Souls," "The Eyes,"
           "Afterward," "The Lady's Maid's Bell," "Kerfol," "The Triumph

of Night," "Miss Mary Pask," "Bewitched," "Mr. Jones,"
"Pomegranate Seed," and "A Bottle of Perrier."

1938

March

"A Little Girl's New York" [autobiographical article], *Harper's Magazine*, 176: 356–64.

1939

October

Eternal Passion in English Poetry (New York and London: Appleton-Century). A collection of love poems selected by Edith and Robert Norton, with the collaboration of Gaillard Lapsley, and with a "Preface" by Edith (pp. v–vii).

A Wharton Who's Who

Adams, Henry (1838–1918), American historian and man of letters. After knowing each other for many years, their friendship essentially began in 1908 as Adams often then and thereafter visited Paris, especially to see Elizabeth Cameron, a friend of Edith's. He came to feel very close to the Americans whom he knew in Paris, and felt that Edith was one of the most central of them. Special mutual friends were "Bay" Lodge, whose biography Adams published in 1911, Walter Berry, and Daisy Chanler.

Bahlmann, Anna (d. 1916), Edith met her early in the 1870's in Newport and later in New York City, where Edith studied German and German literature under her tuition. In *A Backward Glance*, Edith speaks of her as "my beloved German teacher, who saw which way my fancy turned, and fed it with all the wealth of German literature, from the Minnesingers to Heine" (p. 48). About 1904 Edith hired her as a secretary and literary assistant in dealings with publishers. She lived with the Whartons at 882 Park Avenue, and then in January 1910 joined them in Paris as Edith's secretary and companion.

Berenson, Bernard (1865–1959), American art historian. He graduated in 1887 from Harvard, where he studied art history under Charles Eliot Norton. Berenson was a very close friend of Edith's to whom she wrote numerous letters, often saw in Paris and London, often had as a guest, often visited, and often travelled with him. Their friendship began as Henry Adams brought them together at Voisin's in Paris in 1909 and continued until her death. She dedicated a volume of short stories, *Human Nature*, to him in 1933. She was also a close friend of his wife, Mary, and his professional associate, Nicky Mariano.

Berenson, Mary (1864–1945), American wife of the art historian. The former Mary Pearsall Smith, she was sister of Logan Pearsall Smith, and became a friend of Edith's, who often visited her and her husband at their home overlooking Florence, I Tatti.

Berry, Walter Van Rensselaer (1859–1927), American lawyer. He graduated from Harvard in 1881 and first met Edith in 1883 in Bar Harbor, Maine, where they became very close. He established a career in Washington and came to specialize in international law. He and Edith reestablished their connection in July 1897, as he visited her at Land's

End and gave her detailed advice about the book she was doing with Ogden Codman about the decoration of houses. She later said that he taught her never to be satisfied with her own work, but also never to surrender her inner conviction to outside opinion. From 1908 to 1910, he was a judge on the International Tribunal in Cairo, but afterwards he settled in Paris, saw a great deal of Edith, and travelled extensively with her, both delivering supplies to the front lines during the First World War, and afterwards in Morocco and especially in southern Europe. During the War he was president of the American Chamber of Commerce in Paris. Edith arranged to have his ashes interred in the Cimetiére des Gonards in Versailles and was buried close to his grave. She wrote a memorial poem for him, "Garden Valedictory," that was published in *Scribner's Magazine*.

Blanche, Jacques Emile (1861–1942), French portrait painter and man of letters. In *A Backward Glance*, Edith spoke of the bilingual Blanche as "One of the first friends I made . . . , in whose house one met not only most of the worthwhile in Paris, but an interestimg admixture of literary and artistic London. . . . Blanche, besides being an excellent linguist, and a writer of exceptional discernment on contemporary art, is also a cultivated musician" (pp. 283, 285), and through him she would meet with people like Diaghilev, George Moore, André Gide, and Jean Cocteau. She often visited him and his wife near Paris, and in 1908 commissioned him to do a portrait of Henry James. Blanche also contributed to *The Book of the Homeless*.

Bliss, Mildred Barnes (1879–1969), wife of Robert Woods Bliss. She worked together with Edith in Paris on war relief projects, and accompanied her and Walter Berry on drives to the war front. Later, she joined with her husband in an attempt to secure the 1927 Nobel Prize for Edith.

Bliss, Robert Woods (1875–1962), American diplomat. In 1912 he became Secretary of the American Embassy in Paris. In 1920 he and his wife purchased the Dumbarton Oaks estate in Washington, D.C., to the enhancement of which Edith's niece, Beatrix Farrand, devoted years of gardening effort. In 1926, while American Ambassador to Sweden, Bliss and his wife tried to obtain the 1927 Nobel Prize for Edith.

Boccon-Gibod, André (n. d.), Parisian lawyer who helped Edith obtain her divorce from Teddy. During World War I he was legal counsel for the American Hostels for Refugees. In 1927 he helped Edith buy the Chateau Ste. Claire. Edith asked that he be a pallbearer at her funeral, which he did.

Bourget, Minnie David (c. 1866–1933), wife of Paul Bourget. In the autumn of 1893, when the Bourgets were visiting America, they called upon Edith and Teddy in Newport with a letter of introduction to her from a cousin of Teddy's mother in Paris. Here their friendship began. Later in Paris, Minnie collaborated with Edith in preparing a French translation of Edith's short story, "The Muse's Tragedy," which then appeared in the July 1900 issue of the *Revue hebdomadaire*.

Bourget, Paul (1852–1935), French novelist, essayist, and Academician. The Bourgets had gone to America in 1893 in order for Paul to gather material for a series of articles for the *New York Herald*, later collected in his book, *Outre-Mer*. They stayed for two weeks in Newport, visited Edith and Teddy frequently at Land's End, and began what would be a long and important friendship. Recalling in *A Backward Glance* the meeting, Edith wrote of it as the start of "a friendship as close with the brilliant and stimulating husband as with his quiet and exquisite companion" (p. 103). Beginning two months later, they repeatedly met in Europe and vacationed together, notably in August 1899, when they travelled in northern Italy on what Edith in *A Backward Glance* called an "enchanting journey, which I afterward sketched in . . .'Italian Backgrounds.' " The experience also "was soon to result in the writing of my first novel, 'The Valley of Decision' " (p. 105), which she dedicated to them "In Remembrance of Italian Days." Later, they saw a great deal of each other in Paris, where he "smoothed my social path" (p. 264), and at Costabelle, where the Bourgets had a home near Edith's at Hyéres. He gave her a letter of introduction to Violet Paget in Florence, who helped Edith prepare *Italian Villas and Their Gardens*. Bourget also contributed to *The Book of the Homeless*.

Brownell, William Crary (1851–1928), American editor, literary critic, and journalist, who was a senior literary consultant for Scribner, and accepted Edith's first book, *The Decoration of Houses*, for publication, as well as subsequent works. In *A Backward Glance*, Edith called him "Our most distinguished man of letters, . . . and though he became a dear friend it was chiefly by letter that we communicated" (p. 144). When he died, she wrote a memorial article for him that was published in *Scribner's Magazine*.

Burlingame, Edward L. (1848–1922), Brownell's colleague at Scribner, and editor of *Scribner's Magazine* from 1887 to 1914. When Edith submitted her poem, "The Last Giustiniani," the letter of acceptance was sent by Burlingame, who became, Edith wrote in *A Backward Glance*, "one of my most helpful guides in the world of letters. He not only accepted my verses, but (oh, rapture!) wanted to know what else I had written; and this encouraged me to go to see him, and laid the foundation of a friendship which lasted till his death" (p. 109). He also accepted Edith's first work of fiction to be published, "Mrs. Manstey's View," which was followed by many other publications in *Scribner's Magazine*. She dedicated *The Descent of Man and Other Stories* to him, calling him "my first and kindest critic."

Chanler, Margaret Terry ("Daisy") (n. d.), She was born in Rome, the daughter of Luther Terry, the American expatriate painter, who was a friend of Edith's father. She and Edith first met in 1867 as children playing in Rome on the Monte Pincio. In 1886 she married Winthrop Astor Chanler and lived in Newport, where she renewed her acquaintance with Edith, who became a very close friend. In 1902 Edith attended the christening in Newport of Daisy's son Theodore, who was named after President Roosevelt, who was also present at the ceremony. Daisy and her husband visited Edith in Paris and at Ste. Claire, and were passengers on Edith's rented yacht, the *Osprey*, in 1926. Daisy and Edith also had an extensive correspondence.

Clark, Kenneth (1903–83), British art scholar and curator. While driving in Italy during the autumn of 1930 with Bernard Berenson and Nicky Mariano, Edith met Clark, who had been a protégé of Berenson's, having come with his bride, Jane, in 1927 to Settignano to study art history under Berenson's guidance. He soon became a much valued friend of Edith's, who in 1932 became godmother to Kenneth and Jane's son, Colin. They often visited each other in England and at Edith's two homes, Ste. Claire and the Pavillon Colombe. Edith asked that he be a pallbearer at her funeral, which he did. He also was given much of her library.

Codman, Ogden, Jr. ("Coddy") (1868–1951), American architect and interior designer. He studied in France and at the Massachusetts Institute of Technology, and established his practice in his native city of Boston. After buying Land's End in 1893, Edith extensively consulted with Codman on how to redesign its interior. She also co-authored with him *The Decoration of Houses* (1897). When she decided to build The Mount, she again turned to Codman, but his fees were so high that she chose another architect. Years later Codman moved to France, where they remained in touch and where he bought a chateau south of Paris. Here she stopped on her last journey north from Ste. Claire to St. Brice, and here in early June 1937 she had a stroke and had to be transported by ambulance to the Pavillon Colombe.

Du Bos, Charles (n. d.), French literary critic and biographer. Paul Bourget chose Du Bos, who was English on his mother's side, to translate *The House of Mirth*, which Du Bos very much admired. During the course of translating it, Edith recalled in A *Backward Glance*, Du Bos "became one of my closest friends" (p. 286). In 1906 it began to appear as *La Demeure de liesse* in the *Revue de Paris*, and was published in book form as *Chez les Heureux du Monde*. During the wartime influx of French and Belgian refugees into Paris, Du Bos, with French and Belgian friends, organized a relief committee, L'Accueil France-Belge, but as it became overstrained Edith was asked to form an American relief committee. Later Du Bos published a biography of Byron in French (1929), afterwards translated into English and published in New York and London as *Byron and The Need of Fatality* (1932).

Farrand, Beatrix Jones (1872–1959), Edith's niece, the daughter of Frederic and Mary Cadwallader Jones. She helped Edith with the gardens at The Mount. Edith was very close to Mary and Beatrix, and sailed to New York in December 1913 to attend Beatrix's wedding to Max Farrand, a professor of American history at Yale. Beatrix became an outstanding landscape gardener, and did important work in the United States, including gardens at Dumbarton Oaks for Robert and Mildred Bliss, and in England, designing the gardens at Glyndebourne.

Fullerton, William Morton (1865–1952), American journalist. He was a member of the class of 1886 at Harvard, where he studied with Charles Eliot Norton and became a friend of the Norton family, and where he met Bernard Berenson. Fullerton came to London in about 1890, secured a position with the *Times*, and soon met Henry James, with whom he was to have a long, warm friendship. He also had an affair with Margaret Brooke, the Ranee of Sarawak. In 1902 the *Times* transferred him to their bureau in Paris, where he became their major correspondent, and had a very active love life. By the spring of 1907 he had met Edith, and soon helped to arrange serial publication of the Du Bos translation of *The House of Mirth* in the *Revue de Paris*, for which he was writing a series of articles on the Rhone Valley. They often saw each other and in October 1907, while visiting America to see his family, he stayed for several days at The Mount, where he and Edith became very close. A few days after his departure, Edith began a private journal addressed to Fullerton. Back in Paris they saw a good deal of each other and in May 1908 began an intimate relationship that lasted until 1911, after which they continued as friends. Fullerton, who had left the *Times* and become a freelance writer, continued his friendship with Henry James and, prompted by the publication of the New York Edition of James's works, Fullerton in 1910 published a long article in the *Quarterly Review* (reprinted in the American *Living Age*), that articulated the scope and artistry of James's writing, and was the first critical study to discuss James's place in the history of fiction.

Gay, Matilda (n. d.), Edith had known her since childhood and saw a good deal of her in France, where she lived with her expatriate artist husband, Walter Gay. The Whartons often visited them at their villa, Le Bréau, near Fontainebleau. She was a member of the Franco-American General Committee chaired by Edith, and also served with her husband on Edith's Children of Flanders Rescue Committee.

Gerhardi, William Alexander (1895–1977), English novelist, born in St. Petersburg of a Russian father and an English mother. He studied at Oxford and reflected this dual heritage in his novel, *Futility* (London: 1922), which Edith greatly admired, and which initiated their correspondence and friendship. She arranged for its publication in America by Duffield, and contributed a preface to it. He visited her at Ste. Claire in January 1924, by which time he had also published *Anton Chekov. A Critical Study*.

Gilder, Richard Watson (1844–1909), American poet, journalist, and editor. Gilder edited *Scribner's Monthly* from 1870 to 1881, and *The Century Illustrated Monthly Magazine* from 1881 to 1909. In 1902 he asked Edith to do a series of articles for the *Century* about Italian villas that would be illustrated by Maxfield Parrish. She did so and they were gathered together in her first travel book, *Italian Villas and Their Gardens*.

Gosse, Sir Edmund (1849–1928), literary historian, critical essayist, biographer, and autobiographer. Gosse joined Edith and W. D. Howells in an attempt to get the Nobel Prize for Henry James in 1911, and assisted Percy Lubbock, Hugh Walpole, Lucy Clifford, and others in organizing the 70th birthday tribute to James in 1913.

Howells, William Dean (1837–1920), editor, novelist, critic, and poet. After working in New York for the *Nation* under E. L. Godkin, he moved to Boston in 1866 and became sub-editor of the *Atlantic Monthly* under J. T. Fields, who delegated most of the editorial work to Howells. He served as editor-in-chief from 1871 to 1881. In 1879, a Newport neighbor of the Jones family, Allen Thorndike Rice, sent some of Edith's poems to Henry Wadsworth Longfellow, who passed them on to Howells. He chose five and published them in the magazine in early 1880. In early 1902 he asked Edith to write an article comparing three versions of the Francesca da Rimini legend; it appeared in the July issue of the *North American Review*. In October 1906 he attended the opening of *The House of Mirth* in New York as Edith's guest. In March 1913 he co-signed with Edith an appeal to American donors for a gift honoring Henry James's 70th birthday, but after James's objection, the proposal was dropped. Several years later he gave her a poem for *The Book of the Homeless*. In 1921

Howells became the first novelist to receive the Gold Medal of the National Institute of Arts and Letters. Edith became the second in 1924.

Hugh Smith, John (b. 1881), English banker. A friend of Percy Lubbock, whom he knew at Cambridge, Robert Norton, Howard Sturgis, and Henry James, Hugh Smith met Edith in December 1908 at Stanway, the country estate of Lord Hugo and Lady Mary Elcho. After several more English meetings, and after Edith's return to Paris, they begin to correspond and grew close. During his first trip to America in July 1911, he stayed at The Mount, along with Henry James and Gaillard Lapsley. Over the years he also visited her at Ste. Claire and the Pavillon Colombe. She said she dedicated *Hudson River Bracketed* to him because he was an excellent critic and had patiently read early proofs of the novel. She asked that he be a pallbearer at her funeral, but he was unable to attend.

Hunter, Mary (d. 1933), an English friend whom Edith loved to visit, beginning in 1913, at her home, Hill Hall, near Epping in Sussex. After the death in 1920 of Howard Sturgis, his home of Queen's Acre, the meeting place of Edith's closest friends in England, was sold, and Hill Hall became its successor for their gatherings. Edith's last stay was in 1924 with Geoffrey Scott, Percy Lubbock, Gaillard Lapsley, and Robert Norton, after which, following the death of Mary's husband, she sold the home and moved to London. In *A Backward Glance*, Edith called her "so much a part of my annual English holiday, so much the centre of my picture of the English world" (p. 297).

James, Henry (1843–1916), a dear friend who was Edith's closest artistic companion. After visiting James in 1902, Edith's sister-in-law, Mary Cadwalader Jones, gave him two volumes of Edith's short stories, and James replied by giving Edith an advance copy of *The Wings of the Dove* and sending her a congratulatory letter regarding *The Valley of Decision*, in which he urged her to favor American subjects. In the following year he went to London to meet her, and their friendship warmly developed. In May 1904 Edith and Teddy visited Lamb House for the first time, and in October he visited them at The Mount, along with Walter Berry and Howard Sturgis. In *A Backward Glance*, where Edith devoted a chapter to James, she spoke of the appropriateness of putting his name first among the closest friends who gathered at The Mount, and evoked his gift of talk that "poured out in a series of images so vivid and appreciations so penetrating, the whole so sunned over by irony, sympathy and wide-flashing fun" (p. 179), that was a sheer delight. He became won over to the pleasure of motoring through the countryside while there, and afterwards went on many trips with them in England, as in 1906, when they visited Howard Sturgis at Queen's Acre, and in France in 1907. During his next visit to Paris, in 1908, by which time he had been addressing her in his letters as "Dear Edith," she arranged for his portrait by Jacques-Emile Blanche. Later that year he expressed his deep distress at her involvement with Morton Fullerton, but she continued her closeness to both men, and became "Dearest Edith" to James in 1909. In 1912 Edith commissioned another portrait of him, this time by John Singer Sargent, and visited him at Lamb House. In the following year he was very upset when he learned of her plan to raise in America a sum of money for his 70th birthday, but though she abandoned that effort she secretly arranged with Scribner to fund an advance payment for his next novel, and rejoiced on learning of his acceptance of the Scribner offer. Though separated by the War, both James and Edith gave assistance to Belgian refugees, and he contributed "The Long Wards" to her *Book of the Homeless* shortly before his death. She called his friendship the pride and honor of her life.

Jewett, Rutger Bleecker (1867–1935), American editor and publisher. Jewett was an editor at Appleton with whom Edith worked for many years, beginning with *The Marne* (1918), which he found a very poignant work, and which was the first of a lengthy series of her books to be published by Appleton. For the next sixteen years he was her editor and, for the last twelve, served as her agent as well, securing serial rights from magazines, advance royalties, and film and dramatic rights. He met her several times in Paris and later paid two visits to Ste. Claire.

Jones, Mary Cadwalader ("Minnie") (1850–1935), Edith's sister-in-law. She had married Freddy Jones in 1870, lived with him at 21 East 11th Street in New York City, and became closely attached to young Edith. In 1872 she had her only child, Beatrix, who would become a famous landscape gardener. Minnie separated from her husband in 1892 and divorced him in 1896 because of his adulterous affairs. She continued to live on 11th Street, and also in a summer home at Reef Point in Bar Harbor, Maine, where Edith visited her. She became a major American contact person for Edith, securing work orders for unemployed Parisian seamstresses in 1914, for example, and then becoming the chair of the New York committee to help carry out the work of the American Hostels for Refugees. After the War, she did research on historical details of old New York for *The Age of Innocence* and became Edith's theatre and cinema representative, reading proofs and working on her own and with Jewett in dealing with agents and producers who wished to present in their media some of Edith's stories and novels. She died suddenly on a visit to England, where Edith had her buried, and then settled her estate.

Lapsley, Gaillard (1871–1949), medieval historian. Born in New England, he graduated from Harvard, and after further study became a fellow and lecturer at Trinity College, Cambridge University. He met Edith in Massachusetts in 1904 while she was on a motor tour with Teddy and Walter Berry, and soon joined them at The Mount. He and Edith developed their friendship on her trips to England, seeing him at Cambridge or in the company of close friends like Henry James and Howard Sturgis. He also motored with her through France and on her trip to North Africa, and visited her when he came to Paris. In 1925 she dedicated *The Writing of Fiction* to him. By then, for some years he had been a regular guest at Hyères and was a member, together with Robert Norton and Edith, of what she in 1926 called the literary committee of Ste. Claire. Her dedication of *The Children* (1928) to her "Patient Listeners at Ste. Claire" included Geoffrey Scott and the Bernard Berensons as well as Lapsley and Norton. She also asked that Lapsley be a pallbearer at her funeral, which he did. As her literary executor, he requested that Percy Lubbock write a memoir of Edith, which became *Portrait of Edith Wharton* (1946).

Lubbock, Percy (1879–1965), English literary critic, novelist, biographer, and editor. At Cambridge University he became friends with Edith's future close associates, Gaillard Lapsley, John Hugh Smith, and Howard Sturgis. He met Edith in 1906, when he, Edith, Teddy, and Henry James were all guests at Howard Sturgis's house, Queen's Acre, near Windsor. She then visited him in England and in 1914 took him with her on her trip through North Africa, together with Gaillard Lapsley. He visited her in Paris and at Ste. Claire, but after his marriage in 1926 to Lady Sybil Cutting, whom Edith detested, her affection for him waned and never revived. In spite of this breach, Gaillard Lapsley, with the support of John Hugh Smith and Bernard Berenson, asked him to write *Portrait of Edith Wharton*.

Mariano, Elizabeth ("Nicky") (n. d.), In 1918, she was hired as a librarian for Bernard Berenson at Villa I Tatti, at Settignano, near Florence. Later she became his personal assistant and companion, staying with Berenson and his wife, Mary, for forty years. Edith met her only briefly in London in 1923, but got to know her better when visiting Settignano later that year, and became fond of her during reunions with Berenson and Nicky while travelling through Italy. They came to Paris to be with her after the death of Walter Berry, and then began to visit Ste. Claire at Christmas. Edith returned to Rome after an absence of seventeen years with Nicky in 1931, and in the following year again went with her to Rome, where they had a memorable time in seeing art and architecture, but also shared an intense responsiveness to the Catholic mass and liturgy. Shortly before Edith's death she asked that her dresses be given to Nicky.

Norton, Charles Eliot (1827–1908), American editor, author, teacher. From 1863 to 1868 he co-edited the *Atlantic Monthly* with James Russell

Lowell, and from 1873 to 1897 was a Professor of Fine Arts at Harvard, where Bernard Berenson was one of his students. He and Edith shared a love of Dante, two of whose works he translated, and he prompted her to read John Donne, whose poems he edited. In *A Backward Glance*, Edith speaks of making moving visits to the library at Norton's home of Shady Hill, near Harvard, from which he helped her do research on 18th century Italy when she was writing *The Valley of Decision*, by which time he had become "one of my great friends" (p. 128). Even more, she often drove from The Mount to his summer home, Ashfield, in northwestern Massachusetts to visit him and his daughters, at times bringing guests like Henry James, Walter Berry, and Gaillard Lapsley, "for my most intimate friends were his friends also" (p. 155). She loved his conversation, which she found wise and humane, and warmly admired "his animating influence on my generation in America" (p. 154). For his 80th birthday, she wrote a sonnet, "High Pasture," that his daughter, Sara, published in her edition of his letters.

Norton, Robert ("Norts") (n. d.), English watercolor painter. Edith met him and John Hugh Smith at Stanway, the country home of Lord and Lady Elcho (later Wemyss) in 1908. After being released from wartime duties with the British Admiralty, he joined Edith in January 1919 on a trip to the Riviera, he to paint and she to find a winter escape from Paris. While staying at Hyères for four months, they became close friends and discovered Ste. Claire, which Edith decided to lease and use as a winter home. Here he came as a Christmas guest for many years. Edith also invited him to take an Aegean cruise with her in 1926, and visited him in England, where he had become the resident custodian of Henry James's former home, Lamb House. He edited *Eternal Passion in English Poetry* with her, and was a pallbearer at her funeral.

Norton, Sara ("Sally") (c. 1864–1922), Of Charles Eliot Norton's children, Edith was closest to Sally, his eldest daughter. Sally, who had met Edith in New York, wrote Edith in praise of *The Touchstone* (1900), thereby beginning what became a regular correspondence that was very loving and intimate. Sally was also a beloved, frequent guest at The Mount, and fondly welcomed Edith at Shady Hill and at Ashfield. In commemoration of their friendship, Edith dedicated her sonnet, "Uses," to Sally.

Paget, Violet ("Vernon Lee") (1856–1935), English historian and art critic. Edith very much admired Paget's book, *Studies of the Eighteenth Century in Italy* (1880), and took it with her on her journeys through Italy. In *A Backward Glance*, Edith called it, and Paget's *Belcaro* and *Euphorion* "three of my best-loved companions of the road" (p. 130).

They met in 1894, when Edith came to Florence, where Paget was living, with a letter of introduction from Paul Bourget. Edith was struck not just by Paget's extensive knowledge of Italian culture, but also by her lively intelligence and cultivated behavior, and they spent hours together. She also met Paget's brother, Eugene Lee-Hamilton, who wrote to her in 1902 after publication of *The Valley of Decision*, expressing his and his sister's great admiration for the book. In the following year, Edith again came to see Paget, seeking her help in gathering material for *Italian Villas and Their Gardens*. Paget gave her great assistance, indicating which villas Edith should see, travelling with her, and securing access for her to those that were private. Accordingly, Edith dedicated her book to Paget.

Scott, Geoffrey (1883–1929), English architect, cultural historian, biographer, and editor. He and Edith met at the home of his Florentine mentor, Bernard Berenson, in 1913, and became friends as they motored together from I Tatti to Paris. In *A Backward Glance*, Edith recalled later meetings in Florence, that led to "many delightful pilgrimages," as they would "go off on architectural excursions and garden hunts . . . all through Tuscany and Umbria" (p. 328). In 1916 he stayed at her Paris home for four months, acting as her secretary and intellectual companion. Over the years they sometimes met in England, as in 1924, on Edith's last visit to Hill House with Percy Lubbock, Gaillard Lapsley, and Robert Norton. Mostly, however, they met in France, where he was her guest at the Pavillon Colombe and at Ste. Claire, where, during the winter of 1927–28, he was one of the "Patient Listeners" as Edith read aloud portions of *The Children* to him, Lapsley, Norton, and Bernard and Mary Berenson. She last saw him in London as he was preparing to leave for America, where he was editing newly-discovered Boswell papers, and where he suddenly died two weeks later.

Simmons, Ronald (c. 1887–1918), American painter whom Edith came to know in Paris, where he was studying and where he began to serve as secretary of the cure program for tubercular French soldiers that she had helped establish. She became very fond of him and characterized his affection for her as like that of a loving younger brother. When America declared war on Germany in April 1917, he volunteered for service and was appointed head of the American Intelligence service in Marseilles, from which he wrote to her and where in August of the following year he died of pneumonia. She wrote an obituary poem, "For R. S.," that was published in *Scribner's Magazine*, and dedicated *The Marne* and *A Son at the Front* to him.

Smith, Logan Pearsall (1865–1946), British essayist and critic. Smith, the brother of Mary Pearsall Smith Berenson, was born in Philadelphia and educated at Haverford College and Harvard University before transferring to Baliol College, Oxford, and becoming a permanant resident of England. Edith met him briefly in Florence in 1903 with his sister and Bernard Berenson, and became friends with him while visiting Howard Sturgis at Queen's Acre in 1911 in the company of Henry James, Gaillard Lapsley, and Percy Lubbock. He was a passenger on Edith's rented boat, the *Osprey*, when they sailed through the Mediterranean and the Aegean in 1926, and was a visitor at Ste. Claire and the Pavillon Colombe.

Sturgis, Howard (1855–1920), writer and man of leisure. The son of an American banker working in England for Baring Brothers, he was born in England, educated at Eton and Cambridge University, and became a permanent resident of England. His friendship with Edith began when she met him in Newport a few years after her marriage and in *A Backward Glance* called it "a case of friendship at first sight" (p. 225). She saw him in England and then again in 1904, when, on another visit to the the United States, he was brought by Henry James to The Mount. He warmly responded to *The House of Mirth* (1905), writing to her and saying that she and Henry James were the best of contemporary novelists. She often visited him at his home of Queen's Acre, near Windsor, and in *A Backward Glance*, said that at his home "some of the happiest hours of my life were passed, some of my dearest friendships formed or consolidated." She called him "one of the most amusing and lovable of companions," and treasured his hospitality to her "inner group" of friends: Percy Lubbock, Gaillard Lapsley, John Hugh Smith, Robert Norton, and Henry James (pp. 230–31).

Tyler, Elisina (Mrs. Royall) (1875–1959), Born in Italy, she spent most of her life in England and France. In 1914 she and her husband moved to Paris, where they volunteered to assist Edith in her wartime charity work. Elisina and Edith quickly became friends, and Elisina served as vice-chairman and frequently acting chairman of the General Committee of the American Hostels for Refugees. She served similarly on the Children of Flanders Rescue Committee, and oversaw the operation of Edith's two American Convalescent Homes, even after the War. For her refugee work, Elisina, like Edith, was given the Médaille Reine Elisabeth by the Belgian government in 1918. She also received the French Legion of Honor, as Edith had in 1916. In 1918, she also discovered the Pavillon Colombe and showed it to Edith, who loved it and bought it. During ensuing years when Edith became seriously ill, as in 1929, 1935, and 1937, Elisina was sent for and rushed to Edith's side, caring for her and managing her household. She came from Rome and was with Edith during her final two months. Edith told her of her wishes regarding her funeral and burial, and made Elisina the executor of her French estate.

Tyler, Royall (n. d.), American scholar and art historian. Edith had met him before the War, but their association began when Tyler and his wife, Elisina, moved to Paris and volunteered to help Edith with her wartime charities. He served as secretary and treasurer of the Children of Flanders Rescue Committee, and as an officer of the American Hostels for Refugees. In *A Backward Glance*, Edith said "Royall Tyler rendered me immense help until our entry into the war enrolled him in the United States Intelligence service" in Paris (p. 348). They remained in close personal contact until the end of her life. He was a pallbearer at her funeral.

Wharton, Edward Robbins ("Teddy") (1850–1928), As a friend of Edith's brother, Harry, he came to know her. After graduating from Harvard in 1873 with an undistinguished academic record, he lived as a leisured bachelor on an allowance from his parents in Boston, which continued until he was 60. He escorted Edith to a Patriarchs' Ball in New York during February 1884, became engaged to her in January 1885, and married her in April of that year. Their sexual relationship was delayed for several weeks and evidently it soon ceased. Their marriage continued on the basis of moderate fondness and a love of social engagements, domestic animals, chiefly little dogs (instead of children), and outdoor activity, notably horseback riding, picnicking, and travel, especially by automobile. For some years they lived at Newport from June until February, and then travelled for four months in Europe, especially Italy. During planning and construction of The Mount in Lenox during 1901–02, he began to show signs of mental disturbance that emulated the unbalanced behavior of his father, ranging from jaunty cheerfulness to restlessness, irritability, and manic depression. In October 1902, shortly after moving into The Mount he suffered the first of what was to be a series of nervous collapses, as his loss of mental health caused physical problems as well, ranging from headaches and facial neuralgia to gout pains and swollen, aching joints. He had another nervous collapse in July 1903 and again in September. For the ensuing four years his health was reasonably stable, but soon after arriving in Paris in December 1907, he fell into a nervous depression. In March of the following year, suffering from gout, he returned to America by himself, going for treatment to Hot Springs, Arkansas. Edith rejoined him for summer at The Mount, but when she left for Paris in October, he stayed in New York and apparently began dallying with actresses. When he came to Paris in January 1909, he was suffering from insomnia, bodily pain, and depression. Returning to America in April, he went to Lenox, where his mother died, leaving him about $67,000 and some land. He went to Paris in November 1909, and in a few weeks was again depressed.

He now confessed that in the summer of the previous year, acting as trustee of Edith's trust funds, he had embezzled money, bought an apartment in Boston, and lived there with a mistress. Accordingly, his brother, William, transferred $50,000 from Teddy's inheritance to one of Edith's trust funds. Teddy returned to Boston in December 1909. Three months later he went to Paris, but nerve doctors were unable to treat his manic-depressive condition. He then spent June and July 1910 in a Swiss sanitorium, but without significant improvement. Edith then decided not to allow him to manage her monetary affairs and household matters, and urged him to go to the American West, which he had wanted to do. She went with him to New York in September 1910, where their friend, Johnson Morton, was preparing to take him on the westward trip, which now had been extended to a trip around the world. In April 1911, he completed the trip, went to Boston for medical treatment, and sought to regain control over Edith's finances. During July with her at The Mount, his sense of humiliation led to fits of rage and verbal abuse of her, that were at times succeeded by tears and cries for forgiveness. To pacify him, she offered him management of The Mount, but not over her trust funds. He responded with rage and insisted that they break up. She then decided to separate from him, but arranged that $500 a month be placed in his Boston bank account, and gave him legal power to rent or sell The Mount. After she left for Paris in September 1911, he sold it. He came to see her in Paris between February and May 1912, their last time together. In October he came to London, telling her not to join him there, then stopped briefly in Paris without notifying her, and went off on a motor tour to Monte Carlo, where he had another affair. Edith then decided to divorce him, and in April 1913 received a French divorce decree based on his adultery in New York, Boston, London, and Monte Carlo. He died in New York City in 1928, leaving his money to the nurse who had been taking care of him. Edith felt grateful that he was finally at peace after so many years of agitation.

Winthrop, Egerton (1839–1916), a cosmopolitan New York socialite, who also had extensive knowledge of literature, the fine arts, and scientific thought. He returned to New York from Paris in 1885, when close association with Edith began. In *A Backward Glance*, she spoke of him as a friend who "directed and systematized my reading. . . . Through him I first came to know the great French novelists and the French historians and literary critics of the day; but his chief gift was to introduce me to the wonder-world of nineteenth century science." She spoke of their friendship of over thirty years as "perhaps the happiest I was to know," and characterized him as "the most perfect of friends" (p. 94).

Bibliography

1878

Fall

Mrs. Jones has a selection of Edith's poems privately printed in Newport. Entitled *Verses*, it contains "Le Viol d'Amour," "Vespers," "Bettine to Goethe," "Spring Song," "Prophesies of Summer," "Song," "Heaven," "Maiden, Arise," "Spring," "May Marian," "Opportunities," "The Last Token," "Raffaelle to the Fornarina," "Chriemhild of Burgundy," "Some Woman to Some Man," "Lines on Chaucer," "What We Shall Say Fifty Years Hence, of Our Fancy-Dress Quadrille," "Nothing More," "June and December," "October," "A Woman I Know," "Daisies," "Impromptu," "Notre Dame des Fleurs," and German translations: "Three Songs from the German of Emanuel Geibel," "Longing" (from the German of Schiller), and "A Song" (freely translated from the German of Rückert).

1879

May

"Only a Child" [poem], *New York World*, p. 5.

1880

February

"The Parting Day" [poem], *Atlantic Monthly*, 45: 194.

March

"Areopagus" [poem], *Atlantic Monthly*, 45: 335.

April

"A Failure" [poem], *Atlantic Monthly*, 45: 464–65.
"Patience" [poem], *Atlantic Monthly*, 45: 548–49.

May

"Wants" [poem], *Atlantic Monthly*, 45: 599.

1889

October

"The Last Giustiniani" [poem], *Scribner's Magazine*, 6: 405–06.

December
"Euryalus" [poem], *Atlantic Monthly*, 64: 761.
"Happiness" [poem], *Scribner's Magazine*, 6: 715.

1891

January
"Botticelli's Madonna in the Louvre" [poem], *Scribner's Magazine*, 9: 74.

February
"The Tomb of Ilaria Giunigi" [poem], *Scribner's Magazine*, 9: 156.

July
"Mrs. Manstey's View" [short story], *Scribner's Magazine*, 10: 117–22.

November
"The Sonnet" [poem], *The Century Magazine*, 43: 113.

1892

November
"Two Backgrounds" [poem], *Scribner's Magazine*, 12: 550.

1893

January
"Experience" [poem], *Scribner's Magazine*, 13: 91.

September
"Chartres" [poem], *Scribner's Magazine*, 14: 287.

November
"The Fullness of Life" [short story], *Scribner's Magazine*, 14: 699–704.

1894

May
"That Good May Come" [short story], *Scribner's Magazine*, 15: 629–42.

June
"Life" [poem], *Scribner's Magazine*, 15: 739.

October
"An Autumn Sunset" [poem], *Scribner's Magazine*, 16: 419.

1895

January

"Jade" [poem], *The Century Magazine*, 49: 391.
"A Tuscan Shrine" [travel article], *Scribner's Magazine*, 17: 23–32.

October

"The Lamp of Psyche" [short story], *Scribner's Magazine*, 18: 418–28.

1896

July

"The Valley of Childish Things, and Other Emblems" [short story], *The Century Magazine*, 52: 467–69.

1897

December

The Decoration of Houses (New York: Scribner).

1898

January

"Phaedra" [poem], *Scribner's Magazine*, 23: 68.

June

The Decoration of Houses (London: Batsford).

July

"The One Grief" [poem], *Scribner's Magazine*, 24: 90.

September

Stories By Foreign Authors (New York: Scribner). Edith did three translations: "A Great Day" [from Edmondo de Amicis] pp. 11–34, "It Snows" [from Enrico Castelnuovo] pp. 113–34, and "College Friends" [from Edmondo de Amicis] pp. 137–68.

November

"The Pelican" [short story], *Scribner's Magazine*, 24: 620–29.

1899

January

"The Muse's Tragedy" [short story], *Scribner's Magazine*, 25: 77–84.

March

The Greater Inclination (New York: Scribner). It contains eight short stories: "The Muse's Tragedy," "A Journey," "The Pelican," "Souls Belated," "A Coward," "The Twilight of the God," "A Cup of Cold Water," and "The Portrait."
The Greater Inclination (London: John Lane, The Bodley Head).

1900

January

"April Showers" [short story], *Youth's Companion*, 74: 25–28.

March

"The Touchstone" [novella], *Scribner's Magazine*, 27: 354–72.

April

"The Touchstone," *Scribner's Magazine*, 27: 483–501.
"Frederic Bronson" [letter to the editor], *New York Evening Post*, p. 4.
The Touchstone (New York: Scribner).
A Gift From The Grave [The Touchstone] (London: Murray).

June

" 'Copy': A Dialogue" [short story], *Scribner's Magazine*, 27: 657–63.
"In an Alpine Posting-Inn" [travel article], *Atlantic Monthly*, 85: 794–98.

August

"The Duchess at Prayer" [short story], *Scribner's Magazine*, 28: 153–60.
"The Rembrandt" [short story], *Hearst's International-Cosmopolitan*, 29: 429–37.
"Friends" [short story], *Youth's Companion*, 74: 405–06.
"Friends" *Youth's Companion*, 74: 417–18.

October

"The Line of Least Resistance" [short story], *Lippincott's Magazine*, 66: 559–70.

1901

February

"The Angel at the Grave" [short story], *Scribner's Magazine*, 29: 158–66.
"The Recovery" [short story], *Harper's Magazine*, 102: 468–77.
"More Love Letters of an Englishwoman" [parody], *Bookman*, 12: 562–63.

March

"The Moving Finger" [short story], *Harper's Magazine*, 102: 627–32.

April

Crucial Instances (New York: Scribner). It contains seven short stories: "The Duchess at Prayer," "The Angel at the Grave," "The Recovery," "Copy," "The Rembrandt," "The Moving Finger," and "The Confessional." *Crucial Instances* (London: Murray).

August

"The Blashfields' 'Italian Cities' [review of Edwin H. and Evangeline W. Blashfield's *Italian Cities*]," *Bookman*, 13: 563–64.

September

"Mould and Vase" [poem], *Atlantic Monthly*, 88: 343.

November

"Margaret of Cortona" [poem], *Harper's Magazine*, 103: 884–87.

1902

January

"Sub Umbra Liliorum: An Impression of Parma" [travel article], *Scribner's Magazine*, 31: 22–32.

February

"Uses" [poem], *Scribner's Magazine*, 31: 180.
The Valley of Decision, 2 vols. (New York: Scribner). It is dedicated to Paul and Minnie Bourget: "In Remembrance of Italian Days."

March

"The Sanctuaries of the Pennine Alps" [travel article], *Scribner's Magazine*, 31: 353–64.

April

"*Ulysses: A Drama*, by Stephen Phillips," *Bookman*, 15: 168–70.
The Valley of Decision (London: Murray).

May

"*George Eliot*, by Leslie Stephen," *Bookman*, 15: 247–51.
"The Theatres [Mrs. Fiske's performance in *Tess*]," *The Commercial Advertiser*, p. 9.

June

"The Quicksand" [short story], *Harper's Magazine*, 105: 13–21.
"Artemis to Actæon" [poem], *Scribner's Magazine*, 31: 661–62.

July

"The Three Francescas [essay on plays by Stephen Phillips, Gabriele d'Annunzio, and F. Marion Crawford]," *North American Review*, 175: 17–30.

August

"The Reckoning" [short story], *Harper's Magazine*, 105: 342–55.
"A Midsummer Week's Dream: August in Italy" [travel article], *Scribner's Magazine*, 32: 212–22.

September

"The Bread of Angels" [poem], *Harper's Magazine*, 105: 583–85.

October

Hermann Sudermann, *The Joy of Living (Es Lebe das Leben). A Play in Five Acts* [translation] (New York: Scribner).

November

"The Lady's Maid's Bell" [short story], *Scribner's Magazine*, 32: 549–60.
"Vesalius, in Zante" [poem], *North American Review*, 175: 625–31.

December

"The Mission of Jane" [short story], *Harper's Magazine*, 106: 63–74.

1903

February

"Mr. Paul on the Poetry of Matthew Arnold [review of Herbert W. Paul's *Matthew Arnold*]," *Lamp*, 26: 51–54.
"Picturesque Milan" [travel article], *Scribner's Magazine*, 33: 131–41.

April

"A Torchbearer" [poem], *Scribner's Magazine*, 33: 504–05.
Hermann Sudermann, *The Joy of Living (Es Lebe das Leben). A Play in Five Acts* [translation] (New York: Scribner).

August

"Sanctuary" [novella], *Scribner's Magazine*, 34: 148–62.

September

"Sanctuary," *Scribner's Magazine*, 34: 280–90.

October

"Sanctuary," *Scribner's Magazine*, 34: 439–47.
"The Vice of Reading" [essay], *North American Review*, 177: 513–21.
Sanctuary (New York: Scribner).

November

"Sanctuary," *Scribner's Magazine*, 34: 570–80.
"Italian Villas and Their Gardens. Introduction: Italian Garden-Magic," *The Century Magazine*, 67: 21–24.

"Italian Villas and Their Gardens: Florentine Villas," *The Century Magazine*, 67: 25–33.
Sanctuary (London: Macmillan).

December

"The Dilettante" [short story], *Harper's Magazine*, 108: 139–43.
"Expiation" [short story], *Hearst's International-Cosmopolitan*, 36: 209–22.
"A Venetian Night's Entertainment" [short story], *Scribner's Magazine*, 34: 640–51.
"Italian Villas and Their Gardens: Sienese Villas," *The Century Magazine*, 67: 162–64.

1904

February

"The Other Two" [short story], *Collier's*, 32: 15–17, 20.
"Italian Villas and Their Gardens: Roman Villas," *The Century Magazine*, 67: 562–64, 566, 568–72.

March

"The Descent of Man" [short story], *Scribner's Magazine*, 35: 313–22.

April

"The Letter" [short story], *Harper's Magazine*, 108: 781–89.
"Italian Villas and Their Gardens: Villas Near Rome," *The Century Magazine*, 67: 860–61, 863–64, 868, 870–74.
The Descent of Man And Other Stories (New York: Scribner). It contains nine short stories: "The Descent of Man," "The Mission of Jane," "The Other Two," "The Quicksand," "The Dilettante," "The Reckoning," "Expiation," "The Lady's Maid's Bell," and "A Venetian Night's Entertainment."
The Descent of Man And Other Stories (London: Macmillan). It also contains "The Letter."

August

"The House of the Dead Hand" [short story], *Atlantic Monthly*, 94: 145–60.
"The Last Asset" [short story], *Scribner's Magazine*, 36: 150–68.
"Italian Villas and Their Gardens: Lombard Villas," *The Century Magazine*, 68: 541–54.

October

"Italian Villas and Their Gardens: Villas of Venetia," *The Century Magazine*, 68: 885–95.
"Italian Villas and Their Gardens: Genoese Villas," *The Century Magazine*, 68: 895–902.

November

Italian Villas And Their Gardens, illus. Maxfield Parrish (New York: Century). It is dedicated to Vernon Lee: "Who, Better Than Anyone Else Has Understood And Interpreted The Garden-Magic Of Italy."
Italian Villas And Their Gardens, illus. Maxfield Parrish (London: John Lane, The Bodley Head).

December

"The Pot-Boiler" [short story], *Scribner's Magazine*, 36: 696–712.

1905

January

"The House of Mirth" [novel], *Scribner's Magazine*, 37: 33–43.

February

"The House of Mirth," *Scribner's Magazine*, 37: 143–57.

March

"The House of Mirth," *Scribner's Magazine*, 37: 319–37.

April

"The House of Mirth," *Scribner's Magazine*, 37: 469–86.
Italian Backgrounds [travel sketches], illus. E. C. Peixotto (New York: Scribner).
Italian Backgrounds (London: Macmillan).

May

"The House of Mirth," *Scribner's Magazine*, 37: 549–64.
"Mr. Sturgis's '*Belchamber*,' " *Bookman*, 21: 307–10.

June

"The House of Mirth," *Scribner's Magazine*, 37: 738–53.

July

"The House of Mirth," *Scribner's Magazine*, 38: 81–100.

August

"The House of Mirth," *Scribner's Magazine*, 38: 210–20.

September

"The House of Mirth," *Scribner's Magazine*, 38: 332–49.
"Maurice Hewlett's '*The Fool Errant*," ' *Bookman*, 22: 64–67.
"The Best Man" [short story], *Collier's*, 35: 14–17, 21–22.

October

"The House of Mirth," *Scribner's Magazine*, 38: 445–62.

The House of Mirth, illus. A. B. Wenzell (New York: Scribner).
The House of Mirth (London: Macmillan).

November

"The House of Mirth," *Scribner's Magazine*, 38: 605–17.

December

"The Introducers" [short story], *Ainslee's*, 16: 139–48.

1906

January

"The Introducers," *Ainslee's*, 16: 61–67.

February

"The Hermit and the Wild Woman" [short story], *Scribner's Magazine*, 39: 145–56.

April

"In Trust" [short story], *Appleton's Booklover's Magazine*, 7: 432–40.

August

"Madame de Treymes" [novella], *Scribner's Magazine*, 40: 167–92.

December

"A Motor-Flight Through France" [travel serial], *Atlantic Monthly*, 98: 733–41.

1907

January

"A Motor-Flight Through France," *Atlantic Monthly*, 99: 98–105.
"The Fruit of the Tree" [novel], *Scribner's Magazine*, 41: 10–23.

February

"A Motor-Flight Through France," *Atlantic Monthly*, 99: 242–46.
"The Fruit of the Tree," *Scribner's Magazine*, 41: 153–66.

March

"The Fruit of the Tree," *Scribner's Magazine*, 41: 269–83.
Madame de Treymes, illus. Alonzo Kimball (New York: Scribner).
Madame de Treymes (London: Macmillan).

April

"The Fruit of the Tree," *Scribner's Magazine*, 41: 414–28.

May

      "The Fruit of the Tree," *Scribner's Magazine*, 41: 620–34.

June

      "The Fruit of the Tree," *Scribner's Magazine*, 41: 717–34.

July

      "The Fruit of the Tree," *Scribner's Magazine*, 42: 89–112.

August

      "The Fruit of the Tree," *Scribner's Magazine*, 42: 197–216.

September

      "The Fruit of the Tree," *Scribner's Magazine*, 42: 357–78.

October

      "The Fruit of the Tree," *Scribner's Magazine*, 42: 447–68.
      The Fruit of the Tree, illus. Alonzo Kimball (New York: Scribner).
      The Fruit of the Tree (London: Macmillan).

November

      "The Fruit of the Tree," *Scribner's Magazine*, 42: 595–613.
      "The Sonnets of Eugene Lee-Hamilton [review of Eugene Lee-Hamilton's *The Sonnets of the Wingless Hours*]," *Bookman*, 26: 251–53.

1908

January

      "The Old Pole Star" [poem], *Scribner's Magazine*, 43: 68.
      "A Second Motor-Flight Through France" [travel serial], *Atlantic Monthly*, 101: 3–9.

February

      "A Second Motor-Flight Through France," *Atlantic Monthly*, 101: 167–73.

March

      "A Second Motor-Flight Through France," *Atlantic Monthly*, 101: 345–52.

April

      "A Second Motor-Flight Through France," *Atlantic Monthly*, 101: 474–82.

June

      "The Verdict" [short story], *Scribner's Magazine*, 43: 689–93.

July

      "Moonrise Over Tyringham" [poem], *The Century Magazine*, 76: 356–57.

August
> "The Pretext" [short story], *Scribner's Magazine*, 44: 173–87.

September
> *The Hermit and the Wild Woman and Other Stories* (New York: Scribner). It contains seven short stories: "The Hermit and the Wild Woman," "The Last Asset," "In Trust," "The Pretext," "The Verdict," "The Pot-Boiler," and "The Best Man."
>
> *The Hermit and the Wild Woman and Other Stories* (London: Macmillan).

October
> "Les Metteurs en Scène" [short story], *Revue des Deux Mondes*, 67: 692–708.
>
> "Life" [poem], *Atlantic Monthly*, 102: 501–04.
>
> *A Motor-Flight Through France* (New York: Scribner).
>
> *A Motor-Flight Through France* (London: Macmillan).

November
> "The Choice" [short story], *The Century Magazine*, 77: 32–40.

1909

January
> "All Souls' " [poem], *Scribner's Magazine*, 45: 22–23.

March
> "The Bolted Door" [short story], *Scribner's Magazine*, 45: 288–308.

April
> *Artemis to Actæon and Other Verse* (New York: Scribner). It contains 25 poems: "Artemus to Actæon," "Life," "Vesalius in Zante," "Margaret of Cortona," "A Torchbearer," "The Mortal Lease," "Experience," "Grief," "Chartres," "Two Backgrounds," "The Tomb of Ilaria Giunigi," "The One Grief," "The Eumenides," "Orpheus," "An Autumn Sunset," "Moonrise Over Tyringham," "All Souls," "All Saints," "The Old Pole Star," "A Grave," "Non Dolet," "A Hunting-Song," "Survival," "Uses," and "A Meeting."
>
> *Artemis to Actæon and Other Verse* (London: Macmillan).

June
> "His Father's Son" [short story], *Scribner's Magazine*, 45: 657–65.
>
> "A Grave" [poem], *Current Literature*, 46: 685.

July
> "The Daunt Diana" [short story], *Scribner's Magazine*, 46: 35–41.

August
> "The Debt" [short story], *Scribner's Magazine*, 46: 165–72.

October

"Full Circle" [short story], *Scribner's Magazine*, 46: 408–19.

December

"Ogrin the Hermit" [poem], *Atlantic Monthly*, 104: 844–48.

1910

January

"Afterward" [short story], *The Century Magazine*, 79: 321–39.

February

"George Cabot Lodge" [article], *Scribner's Magazine*, 47: 236–39.

March

"The Legend" [short story], *Scribner's Magazine*, 47: 278–91.

June

"The Eyes" [short story], *Scribner's Magazine*, 47: 671–80.

August

"The Letters" [short story], *The Century Magazine*, 80: 485–92.

September

"The Blond Beast" [short story], *Scribner's Magazine*, 48: 291–304.
"The Letters," *The Century Magazine*, 80: 641–50.

October

"The Letters," *The Century Magazine*, 80: 812–19.
Tales of Men and Ghosts (New York: Scribner). It contains ten short stories: "The Bolted Door," "His Father's Son," "The Daunt Diana," "The Debt," "Full Circle," "The Legend," "The Eyes," "The Blond Beast," "Afterward," and "The Letters."
Tales of Men and Ghosts (London: Macmillan).

December

"The Comrade" [poem], *Atlantic Monthly*, 106: 785–87.

1911

March

"Summer Afternoon (Bodiam Castle, Sussex)" [poem], *Scribner's Magazine*, 49: 277–78.

July

"Other Times, Other Manners" [short story], *The Century Magazine*, 82: 344–52.

August

"Other Times, Other Manners," *The Century Magazine*, 82: 587–94.
"Ethan Frome" [novel], *Scribner's Magazine*, 50: 151–64.

September

"Ethan Frome," *Scribner's Magazine*, 50: 317–34.
Ethan Frome (New York: Scribner).
Ethan Frome (London: Macmillan).

October

"Ethan Frome," *Scribner's Magazine*, 50: 431–44.

December

"Xingu" [short story], *Scribner's Magazine*, 50: 684–96.

1912

February

"The Long Run" [short story], *Atlantic Monthly*, 109: 145–63.

March

"Pomegranate Seed" [poem], *Scribner's Magazine*, 51: 284–91.

November

The Reef (New York: Appleton).
The Reef (London: Macmillan).

1913

January

"The Custom of the Country" [novel], *Scribner's Magazine*, 53: 1–24.

February

"The Custom of the Country," *Scribner's Magazine*, 53: 186–206.

March

"The Custom of the Country," *Scribner's Magazine*, 53: 373–95.

April

"The Custom of the Country," *Scribner's Magazine*, 53: 439–54.

May

"The Custom of the Country," *Scribner's Magazine*, 53: 635–53.

June

"The Custom of the Country," *Scribner's Magazine*, 53: 756–74.

July

"The Custom of the Country," *Scribner's Magazine*, 54: 57–74.

August

"The Custom of the Country," *Scribner's Magazine*, 54: 256–67.

September

"The Custom of the Country," *Scribner's Magazine*, 54: 368–76.

October

"The Custom of the Country," *Scribner's Magazine*, 54: 471–83.
The Custom of the Country (New York: Scribner).
The Custom of the Country (London: Macmillan).
Letters of Charles Eliot Norton With Biographical Comment By His Daughter Sara Norton and M.A. De Wolfe Howe, 2 vols. (Boston and New York: Houghton Mifflin). Edith's poem, "High Pasture," appears on Vol. 2, p. 387.

November

"The Custom of the Country," *Scribner's Magazine*, 54: 622–47.

1914

March

A Village Romeo And Juliet. A Tale By Gottfried Keller. Translated By A. C. Bahlmann. With An Introduction By Edith Wharton (New York: Scribner). Edith's introduction appears on pp. v–xxvi.

May

"The Criticism of Fiction" [article], *The Times Literary Supplement*, pp. 229–30.

August

"The Triumph of Night" [short story], *Scribner's Magazine*, 56: 149–62.

December

"Edith Wharton Asks Aid for Destitute Belgians in France" [letter to the editor], *New York Herald*, p. 12.
King Albert's Book. A Tribute To The Belgian King And People From Representative Men And Women Throughout The World (Glasgow: The Daily Telegraph In Conjunction With The Daily Sketch The Glasgow Herald And Hodder And Stoughton). Edith's Poem, "Belgium," appears on p. 165.

1915

January

"Introduction" to Gottfried Keller, *A Village Romeo and Juliet*, trans. A. C. Bahlmann (London: Constable).

May

"The Look of Paris" [article], *Scribner's Magazine*, 57: 523–31.
"The Hymn of the Lusitania" [poem], *New York Herald*, p. 1.
"Jean du Breuil de Saint-Germain" [article], *Revue Hebdomadaire*, 24: 351–61.

June

"In Argonne" [article], *Scribner's Magazine*, 57: 651–60.
"Edith Wharton's Work. She Wants Money to Buy Motors for the French Red Cross" [letter to the editor], *New York Times*, p. 10.

August

"The Great Blue Tent" [poem], *New York Times*, p. 10.

September

"Battle Sleep" [poem], *The Century Magazine*, 90: 736.

October

"In Lorraine and the Vosges" [article], *Scribner's Magazine*, 58: 430–42.

November

"In the North" [article], *Scribner's Magazine*, 58: 600–10.
Fighting France, From Dunkerque to Belfort (New York: Scribner). It contains "The Look of Paris," "In Agonne," "In Lorraine and the Vosges," and "In the North."
Fighting France, From Dunkerque to Belfort (London: Macmillan).
"My Work Among the Women Workers of Paris," *New York Times Magazine*, pp. 1–2.

December

"Coming Home" [short story], *Scribner's Magazine*, 58: 702–18.

1916

January

The Book of the Homeless (New York: Scribner).
The Book of the Homeless (London: Macmillan).

March

"Kerfol" [short story], *Scribner's Magazine*, 59: 329–41.
"Mrs. Wharton's Charity" [letter to the editor], *New York Times*, p. 10.

September

"A New Work for France. Mrs. Wharton on the American Treatment for Tuberculosis" [letter to the editor], *New York Times*, p. 10.

October

"Bunner Sisters" [short story], *Scribner's Magazine*, 60: 439–58.
Xingu And Other Stories. (New York: Scribner). It contains nine short stories: "Xingu," "Coming Home," "Autres Temps . . ." ["Other Times, Other Manners"], "Kerfol," "The Long Run," "The Triumph of Night," "The Choice," and "Bunner Sisters."
Xingu And Other Stories (London: Macmillan).

November

"Bunner Sisters" [short story], *Scribner's Magazine*, 60: 575–96.
"For Tuberculous Soldiers. Mrs. Wharton Explains the Work of the Franco-American Sanatoria" [letter to the editor], *New York Times*, p. 12.

December

"Mrs. Wharton's Appeal" [letter to the editor], *New York Times*, p. 10.

1917

January

"For Mrs. Wharton. Needs of the Work for Tuberculous War Victims" [letter to the editor], *New York Times*, sec. 2, p. 4.
"Mrs. Wharton's Work. Plans of the Committee for 'French Tuberculous War Victims' " [letter to the editor], *New York Times*, p. 8.

February

"Summer" [novella], *McClure's*, 48: 7–8, 10, 51–52.
"From Mrs. Wharton" [letter to the editor], *New York Times*, p. 10.
"For refugees in France" [letter to the editor], *New York Times*, sec. 7, p. 2.

March

"Summer," *McClure's*, 48: 20–22, 62–64.

April

"Summer," *McClure's*, 48: 20–22, 65–67.
"Is There a New Frenchwoman?" [article], *Ladies' Home Journal*, 34: 12, 93.
"Edith Wharton Tells of German Trail of Ruin" [article], *New York Sun*, pp. 1–4.
"For Mrs. Wharton's Work in France" [quoted from a cable to Mary Cadwalader Jones], *New York Times*, p. 12.

May

"Summer," *McClure's*, 49: 20–22, 64–67.
"Mrs. Wharton's Work. The War on Tuberculosis in France – Education of the People" [letter to the editor], *New York Times*, sec. 2, p. 3.

June

"Summer," *McClure's*, 49: 24, 26, 57–60.

July

> "Summer," *McClure's*, 49: 28, 30, 53–57.
> *Summer* (New York: Appleton).
> *Summer* (London: Macmillan).

August

> "Summer," *McClure's*, 49: 31–32, 40–42.

December

> "The French (As Seen by an American)" [article], *Scribner's Magazine*,
> 62: 676–83.

1918

January

> "Les Français vus par une Américaine" [apparently Edith's translation],
> *Revue Hebdomadaire*, 27: 5–21.

March

> "L'Amérique en Guerre" [article], *Revue Hebdomadaire*, 27: 5–28.

August

> "Second Greatest Fourth. So Mrs. Wharton Designates the Celebration
> in Paris This Year" [excerpts from a letter to Mary Cadwalader Jones],
> *New York Times*, p. 10.

October

> "The French We Are Learning to Know" [article], *Hearst's International
> Cosmopolitan*, 65: 32–33, 108–10.
> "The Marne" [novel], *Saturday Evening Post*, 191: 3–5, 74, 77–78, 81–82,
> 85–86, 89–90.

November

> " 'On Active Service'; American Expeditionary Force (R. S., August 12,
> 1918)" [poem], *Scribner's Magazine*, 64: 619.
> [Description of the work of American, Hostels for Refugees], *Heroes of
> France*, no. 2, pp. 2–3.

December

> *The Marne* (New York: Appleton).
> *The Marne. A Tale of the War* (London: Macmillan).

1919

January

> "The Refugees" [short story], *Saturday Evening Post*, 191: 3–5, 53, 57, 61.
> "The Seed of the Faith" [short story], *Scribner's Magazine*, 65: 17–33.

"The French We Are Learning to Know" [article], *Hearst's International Cosmopolitan*, 66: 40–41, 104–06.
"You and You" [poem], *The Pittsburgh Chronicle Telegraph*, p. 6.

February

"How Paris Welcomed the King" [article], *Reveille*, No. 3: 367–69.

March

"The French We Are Learning to Know" [article], *Hearst's International Cosmopolitan*, 66: 40–41, 105–08.
"With the Tide" [poem], *Saturday Evening Post*, 191: 8.

April

"The French We Are Learning to Know" [article], *Hearst's International Cosmopolitan*, 66: 60–61, 94, 96–97.

June

"The French We Are Learning to Know" [article], *Hearst's International Cosmopolitan*, 67: 90–91, 132, 134–36, 138.

July

"Rabat and Salé" [travel serial], *Scribner's Magazine*, 66: 1–16.

August

"Volubilis, Moulay Idriss and Meknez" [travel serial], *Scribner's Magazine*, 66: 131–46.
French Ways and Their Meaning (New York and London: Appleton). It contains "The French We Are Learning to Know," and "Is There a New Frenchwoman?"

September

"Writing a War Story" [short story], *Woman's Home Companion*, 46: 17–19.
"Fez" [travel serial], *Scribner's Magazine*, 66: 324–40.

October

"Marrakech" [travel serial], *Scribner's Magazine*, 66: 473–86.
"Harems and Ceremonies" [travel serial], *Yale Review*, n. s. 9: 47–71.

November

French Ways and Their Meaning (London: Macmillan).

1920

January

"In Provence" [poem], *Yale Review*, n. s. 9: 346–47.
"Lyrical Epigrams" [poem], *Yale Review*, n. s. 9: 348.

July

"Henry James in His Letters [review of Percy Lubbock's *The Letters of Henry James*]," *Quarterly Review*, 234: 188–202.

"The Age of Innocence" [novel], *Pictorial Review*, 21: 5–11, 68, 70, 74, 128.

September

"The Age of Innocence," *Pictorial Review*, 21: 20–26, 92, 95–96, 102–05, 126–35.

In Morocco (New York: Scribner). It is dedicated to General and Madame Lyautey, and contains "Rabat and Salé," "Volubilis, Moulay Idress and Meknez," "Fez," "Marrakech," and "Harems and Ceremonies."

In Morocco (London: Macmillan).

October

"The Age of Innocence," *Pictorial Review*, 22: 23–29, 164–77.

The Age of Innocence (New York and London: Appleton).

November

"The Age of Innocence," *Pictorial Review*, 22: 24–29, 160–64.

1922

February

"The Old Maid" [novella], *The Red Book Magazine*, 38: 31–35, 120–31.

March

"The Old Maid," *The Red Book Magazine*, 38: 37–42, 118–22.

April

"The Old Maid," *The Red Book Magazine*, 38: 46–51, 166, 170.

May

"Glimpses of the Moon" [novel], *Pictorial Review*, 23: 6–11, 73, 92–102.

June

"Glimpses of the Moon," *Pictorial Review*, 23: 17–23, 92–98.

July

"Glimpses of the Moon," *Pictorial Review*, 23: 17–23, 81–82.

The Glimpses of the Moon (New York and London: Appleton).

August

"Glimpses of the Moon," *Pictorial Review*, 23: 17–21, 74–78.

December

"A Son at the Front" [novel], *Scribner's Magazine*, 72: 643–59.

William Gerhardi, *Futility. A Novel On Russian Themes*. Preface By Edith Wharton (New York: Duffield). Edith's preface appears on pp. 1–3.

1923

January

"A Son at the Front," *Scribner's Magazine*, 73: 19–36.

February

"A Son at the Front," *Scribner's Magazine*, 73: 149–66.

March

"A Son at the Front," *Scribner's Magazine*, 73: 259–74.

April

"A Son at the Front," *Scribner's Magazine*, 73: 389–405.

May

"A Son at the Front," *Scribner's Magazine*, 73: 547–55.

June

"A Son at the Front," *Scribner's Magazine*, 73: 688–700.

July

"A Son at the Front," *Scribner's Magazine*, 74: 50–62.
"New Year's Day" [novella], *The Red Book Magazine*, 41: 39–44, 156–64.

August

"A Son at the Front," *Scribner's Magazine*, 74: 169–80.
"New Year's Day," *The Red Book Magazine*, 41: 54–59, 123–24, 126–31.

September

"A Son at the Front," *Scribner's Magazine*, 74: 264–72.
A Son at the Front (New York: Scribner).
A Son at the Front (London: Macmillan).

November

"False Dawn" [novella], *Ladies' Home Journal*, 40: 3–6, 94, 96–97, 99–100, 102, 104–05, 107.

December

"Christmas Tinsel" [autobiographical article], *Delineator*, 103: 11.

1924

February

"Temperate Zone" [short story], *Pictorial Review*, 25: 5–7, 61–62, 64, 66.

May

"The Spark" [novella], *Ladies' Home Journal*, 41: 3–5, 113–16, 119–22.
Old New York [novellas], decorations by E. C. Caswell, 4 vols. (New York and London: Appleton). The four novellas were *False Dawn (The 'Forties), The Old Maid (The 'Fifties), The Spark (The 'Sixties)*, and *New Year's Day (The 'Seventies)*.

October

"The Mother's Recompense" [novel], *Pictorial Review*, 26: 5–9, 28–30, 128.

November

"The Mother's Recompense," *Pictorial Review*, 26: 23–27, 54–56, 59–60, 62.

December

"The Mother's Recompense," *Pictorial Review*, 26: 21–25, 60, 62, 64, 67–68, 70.
"In General" [article], *Scribner's Magazine*, 76: 571–77.

1925

January

"The Mother's Recompense," *Pictorial Review*, 26: 21–25, 31–32, 34.
"Marcel Proust" [article], *Yale Review*, n. s. 14: 209–22.

February

"The Mother's Recompense," *Pictorial Review*, 26: 21–25, 118–19, 120–30.

March

"Bewitched" [short story], *Pictorial Review*, 26: 14–16, 60–64, 69.

April

"Miss Mary Pask" [short story], *Pictorial Review*, 26: 8–9, 75–76.
"Telling a Short Story" [article], *Scribner's Magazine*, 77: 344–49.
The Mother's Recompense (New York and London: Appleton).

May

"Constructing a Novel" [article], *Scribner's Magazine*, 77: 456–61.

June

"Constructing A Novel" [article], *Scribner's Magazine*, 77: 611–19.

August

"Velvet Ear-Muffs" [short story], *The Red Book Magazine*, 45: 39–45, 140–48.

October

"Character and Situation in the Novel" [article], *Scribner's Magazine*, 78: 394–99.

The Writing of Fiction (New York and London: Scribner). It was dedicated to Gaillard Lapsley and contains "In General," "Telling a Short Story," "Constructing a Novel," "Character and Situation in the Novel," and "Marcel Proust."

1926

February

"The Young Gentlemen" [short story], *Pictorial Review*, 27: 29–30, 84–91.

March

Here and Beyond, decorations by E. C. Caswell (New York and London: Appleton). It contains six short stories: "Miss Mary Pask," "The Young Gentlemen," "Bewitched," "The Seed of the Faith," "The Temperate Zone," and "Velvet Ear-Pads."

"A Bottle of Evian" [short story], *Saturday Evening Post*, 198: 8–10, 116, 121–22.

October

Twelve Poems (London: Medici Society). It contains "Nightingales in Florence," "Mistral in the Maquis," "Les Salettes [December 1923]," "Dieu d'Amour [A Castle in Cyprus]," "Segesta," "The Tryst [1914]," "Battle Sleep," "Elegy [1918]," "With the Tide [6th January 1919]," "La Folle du Logis," "The First Year [All Souls' Day]," and "Alternative Epitaphs."

1927

February

"Twilight Sleep" [novel], *Pictorial Review*, 28: 8–11, 78–94.

March

"Twilight Sleep," *Pictorial Review*, 28: 19–21, 96–110.

April

"Twilight Sleep," *Pictorial Review*, 28: 14–15, 85–102.

May

"Twilight Sleep," *Pictorial Review*, 28: 24–25, 91–92, 94, 97, 104, 120–28.

Twilight Sleep (New York and London: Appleton).

July

"The Great American Novel" [article], *Yale Review*, n. s. 16: 646–56.

November

"Atrophy" [short story], *Ladies' Home Journal*, 44: 8–9, 220–22.

1928

January

"Garden Valedictory" [poem], *Scribner's Magazine*, 83: 81.

April

"Mr. Jones" [short story], *Ladies' Home Journal*, 45: 3–5, 108, 111–12, 114, 116.
"The Children" [novel], *Pictorial Review*, 29: 11–16, 60–78.

May

"After Holbein" [short story], *Saturday Evening Post*, 200: 6–7, 179, 181–82, 185–86, 189.
"The Children," *Pictorial Review*, 29: 24–29, 56, 61–70.

June

"The Children," *Pictorial Review*, 29: 25–30, 45–57.

July

"The Children," *Pictorial Review*, 29: 22–25, 68, 82–87.

August

"Had I Been Only" [poem], *Scribner's Magazine*, 84: 215.
"The Children," *Pictorial Review*, 29: 22–25, 64–72.

September

"Hudson River Bracketed" [novel], *Delineator*, 113: 12–14, 88–96.
The Children (New York and London: Appleton).

October

"Dieu d'Amour" [short story], *Ladies' Home Journal*, 45: 6–7, 216, 219–20, 223–24.
"Hudson River Bracketed," *Delineator*, 113: 16–17, 76–85.

November

"William C. Brownell" [article], *Scribner's Magazine*, 84: 596–602.
"Hudson River Bracketed," *Delineator*, 113: 18–19, 101–08.
"A Cycle of Reviewing" [article], *Spectator*, 141, supplement, pp. 44–45.

December

"Hudson River Bracketed," *Delineator*, 113: 16–17, 64–74.

1929

January
"Hudson River Bracketed," *Delineator*, 114: 15–16, 68–73.

February
"Hudson River Bracketed," *Delineator*, 114: 20–21, 101–05.

March
"Hudson River Bracketed," *Delineator*, 114: 25–26, 83, 89.
"Visibility in Fiction" [article], *Yale Review*, n. s. 18: 480–88.

April
"Hudson River Bracketed," *Delineator*, 114: 25, 70–79.

May
"Hudson River Bracketed," *Delineator*, 114: 37–38, 108–13.

June
"Hudson River Bracketed," *Delineator*, 114: 37–38, 58–65.

July
"Hudson River Bracketed," *Delineator*, 115: 34, 83–87.

August
"Hudson River Bracketed," *Delineator*, 115: 35–36, 54.

September
"Hudson River Bracketed," *Delineator*, 115: 49, 105–08.

October
"Hudson River Bracketed," *Delineator*, 115: 41, 117–19.

November
"Hudson River Bracketed," *Delineator*, 115: 49, 102–04.
Hudson River Bracketed (New York and London: Appleton).

December
"Hudson River Bracketed," *Delineator*, 115: 44, 90–93.

1930

January
"Hudson River Bracketed," *Delineator*, 116: 38, 83–85.

February

"Hudson River Bracketed," *Delineator*, 116: 44, 84–96.

October

Certain People (New York and London). It was dedicated to Edward Sheldon, and contains six short stories: "Atrophy," "A Bottle of Perrier," "After Holbein," "Dieu d'Amour," "The Refugees," and "Mr. Jones."

November

"Diagnosis" [short story], *Ladies' Home Journal*, 47: 8–9, 156, 159–60, 162.

1931

April

"Pomegranate Seed" [short story], *Saturday Evening Post*, 203: 6–7, 109, 112, 116, 119, 121, 123.

1932

February

"Her Son" [short story], *Scribner's Magazine*, 91: 65–72, 113–28.
"The Gods Arrive" [novel], *Delineator*, 120: 8–9, 40–42, 45–46, 48, 50.

March

"The Gods Arrive," *Delineator*, 120: 10–11, 66–68, 70, 72, 74, 76, 78.

April

"The Gods Arrive," *Delineator*, 120: 16–17, 78–83, 94.

May

"The Gods Arrive," *Delineator*, 120: 18–19, 89–91, 93–97.

June

"The Gods Arrive," *Delineator*, 120: 12–13, 74–81.

July

"The Gods Arrive," *Delineator*, 120: 12–14, 53–55, 64–67.

August

"The Gods Arrive," *Delineator*, 120: 18–19, 52–53, 60–64.

September

"The Writing of *Ethan Frome*" [article], *Colophon*, part II, no. 4, n. p.
The Gods Arrive (New York and London: Appleton).

November

"A Glimpse" [short story], *Saturday Evening Post*, 205: 16–17, 64–65, 67, 70, 72.

December

"Joy in the House" [short story], *Nash's Pall Mall Magazine*, 90: 6–9, 72–75.

1933

January

"In a Day" [short story], *Woman's Home Companion*, 60: 7–8, 46.

February

"In a Day," *Woman's Home Companion*, 60: 15–16, 104, 106, 118.

March

Human Nature (New York and London: Appleton). It contains five short stories: "Her Son," "The Day of the Funeral" ["In a Day"], "A Glimpse," "Joy in the House," and "Diagnosis."

April

"Confessions of a Novelist" [autobiographical article], *Atlantic Monthly*, 151: 385–92.

October

"A Backward Glance" [autobiographical article], *Ladies' Home Journal*, 50: 5–6, 131–32, 134–37.

November

"A Backward Glance," *Ladies' Home Journal*, 50: 16–17, 90, 92–93, 95.

December

"A Backward Glance," *Ladies' Home Journal*, 50: 15–16, 69.
"The Looking-Glass" [short story], *Hearst's International-Cosmopolitan*, 95: 32–35, 157–59.

1934

January

"A Backward Glance," *Ladies' Home Journal*, 51: 19, 73, 78, 80.
"Tendencies in Modern Fiction" [article], *Saturday Review of Literature*, 10: 433–34.

February

"Bread Upon the Waters" [short story], *Hearst's International-Cosmopolitan*, 96: 28–31, 90, 92, 94, 96, 98.

February–March
"A Backward Glance," *Ladies' Home Journal*, 51: 23, 90, 95, 97.

April
"A Backward Glance," *Ladies' Home Journal*, 51: 49–50, 52, 54, 56.
"Permanent Values in Fiction" [article], *Saturday Review of Literature*, 10: 603–04.
A Backward Glance (New York and London: Appleton-Century).

October
"A Reconsideration of Proust" [article], *Saturday Review of Literature*, 11: 233–34.

November
"Roman Fever" [short story], *Liberty*, 11: 10–14.

1935

April
"Poor Old Vincent!" [short story], *The Red Book Magazine*, 64: 20–23, 116–19.

1936

March
"Unconfessed Crime" [short story], *Story-Teller*, 58: 64–85.

April
The World Over (New York and London: Appleton-Century). It contains seven short stories: "Charm Incorporated," "Pomegranate Seed," "Permanent Wave," "Confession," "Roman Fever," "The Looking-Glass," and "Duration."

June
"Souvenirs du Bourget d'Outre-mer" [article], *Revue Hebdomadaire*, 45: 266–86.

1937

October
Ghosts (New York and London: Appleton-Century). It contains "Preface" and eleven short stories: "All Souls," "The Eyes," "Afterward," "The Lady's Maid's Bell," "Kerfol," "The Triumph of Night," "Miss Mary Pask," "Bewitched," "Mr. Jones," "Pomegranate Seed," and "A Bottle of Perrier."

1938

March

"A Little Girl's New York" [autobiographical article], *Harper's Magazine*, 176: 356–64.

September

The Buccaneers (New York and London: Appleton-Century). An incomplete novel, with Edith's scenario and "A Note" by Gaillard Lapsley (pp. 372–74).

1939

October

Eternal Passion in English Poetry (New York and London: Appleton-Century). A collecion of love poems selected by Edith and Robert Norton, with the collaboration of Gaillard Lapsley, and with a "Preface" by Edith (pp. v–vii).

1968

The Collected Short Stories of Edith Wharton, ed. R. W. B. Lewis (New York: Scribner).

1977

Fast and Loose [novella], ed. Viola Hopkins Winner, (Charlottesville: University of Virginia Press). It was written by Edith in 1876–77 and was not intended for publication.

1981

The House of Mirth, dramatized by Edith Wharton and Clyde Fitch, 1906, ed. Glenn Loney (Rutherford: Farleigh Dickinson University Press; London and Toronto: Associated University Presses).

1988

The Letters of Edith Wharton, ed. R. W. B. Lewis and Nancy Lewis (New York: Scribner).

1990

Stephen Garrison, *Edith Wharton. A Descriptive Bibliography* (Pittsburgh: University of Pittsburgh Press).

Index

Adams, Brooks, 24
Adams, Henry, 21, 42, 51, 95
Akins, Zöe, 89
Allart, Hortense, 36
American Academy of Arts and Letters, 74
American Civil War, 8
American Hostels for Refugees, 56, 59, 96, 102, 107
Anderson, Judith, 89
Appleton and Co., 49, 65, 88, 102
Arthur, Chester A., 11
Asquith, Cynthia, 91
Asquith, Herbert, 91
Astor, William Waldorf, 39
Astor, Mrs. William Waldorf, 39

Bach, Johann Sebastian
    Well-Tempered Clavier, 54
Bahlmann, Anna, 25, 42, 44, 60, 95, 122
    A Village Romeo and Juliet [translation], 54, 56, 122
Bakst, Leon, 59
Balfour, Arthur James, Lord, 76
Barnes, Margaret, 79
Barrie, James, 39, 83
Beerbohm, Max, 39, 59, 91
Beethoven, Ludwig van, 54
Berenson, Bernard, 42, 45, 47–55, 61, 63, 65–71, 73, 78, 81, 83–90, 92, 95, 98–9, 103–6
Berenson, Mary (Mrs. Bernard), 48, 50–2, 73, 78, 82–4, 88, 92, 95, 103, 105–6
Bergson, Henri, 54
Berry, Walter Van Rensselaer, 12, 18, 24, 29–31, 33, 37–9, 41, 44–5, 47–9, 51–7, 62, 68–9, 75–8, 91–2, 95–6, 101, 103–4
Blanche, Jacques-Emile, 37, 50, 59, 61, 96, 102
Blanche, Mrs. Jacques-Emile, 50, 96
Blashfield, Edwin H. and Evangeline W., *Italian Cities*, 23, 113
Bliss, Mildred (Mrs. Robert Woods), 76, 90, 96, 99

Bliss, Robert Woods, 76, 90, 96, 99
Boccon-Gibod, André, 90–1, 96
Boccon-Gibod, Mrs. André, 90
Boer War, 20, 24
Book-of-the-Month Club, 79
Booth, John Wilkes, 8
Bosanquet, Theodora, 58
Boswell, James, 105
Bourget, Paul, 15–16, 20–1, 23, 28, 33, 45, 50, 58–9, 61, 65–6, 76, 96–7, 99, 113
    Outre-Mer, 15, 97
Bourget, Mrs. Paul ("Minnie"), 15–16, 20–1, 23, 28, 50, 58, 65–6, 96–7, 113
Bromfield, Louis, 89
Brooke, Margaret, Ranee of Sarawak, 99
Brooke, Rupert, 59
Brownell, William Crary, 18, 29, 79, 97, 131
Burlingame, Edward, 13–15, 17–18, 28, 97
Butler, Nicholas Murray, 80
Byron, George Gordon, Lord, 99

Café de Paris, 39
Cambon, Jules, 76
Cameron, Elizabeth ("Lizzie"), 59, 95
Campbell, Mrs. Patrick, 24–5
Caswell, E. C., 75, 130
Cecil, Lord David, 83, 91
Chaliapin, Feodor, 53
Chanler, Margaret ("Daisy") (Mrs. Winthrop), 25, 29, 48, 73, 75, 79–81, 83–4, 87, 95, 98
Chanler, Theodore, 25, 98
Chanler, Winthrop Astor, 25, 98
Children of Flanders Rescue Committee, 57, 59, 100, 106–7
Churchill, Winston [American novelist], 31
Cimetière des Gonards, 78, 91–2
Clark, Colette, 85
Clark, Colin, 85, 98
Clark, Jane (Mrs. Kenneth), 82–5, 89–92, 98